T0105660

KINSHIP

KINSHIP

The Dark Secrets of Family Bonds

Jan Sylve

authorHOUSE®

AuthorHouse™
1663 Liberty Drive
Bloomington, IN 47403
www.authorhouse.com
Phone: 1 (800) 839-8640

Published by AuthorHouse 10/30/2015

ISBN: 978-1-5049-5876-9 (sc)
ISBN: 978-1-5049-5875-2 (e)

Print information available on the last page.

This book is dedicated to my father, Arthur Brown Holland, Jr; who taught me to love the outdoors, to cherish my family, and to always stay strong when times seemed really dark. I miss our trips to the beach, picnics with relatives, and camping in the woods.

ACKNOWLEDGMENTS

This book would not have been possible without the love and support of my husband, Robert Sylvester, and my best friend, Judy Nicholson. During the long hours on the computer and the late nights, sometimes doubting my fortitude to continue, they were there.

I would also like to thank my publishing company support team, editorial staff, and the constant support of my publishing coordinator, Brad.

PROLOGUE

Sandy grabbed the sash on Carrie's dress and tore it. Carrie looked at her in disbelief and continued to yell.

"Help me hold her, Sarah. Someone's going to hear." Sarah grabbed Carrie and Sandy gagged her.

"Sarah, we're going to have to tie her up and then go for help. She won't go with us. She doesn't believe us." Sandy tore more of Carrie's dress and tied her feet and arms. "I'm sorry, Carrie. I know you believe they love you, but I heard them talking. You'll be dead after the special ceremony in the woods tonight." As Sandy tried to hold her, Carrie was rolling around and kicking.

Sandy gave Sarah a poncho. "We're going to have to run. Maybe they won't find her in here, but I'm sure someone heard her yelling."

Sandy and Sarah left the cave and Sandy could hear voices not too far away. They both started to run toward the woods.

"Sarah, you stay close to the old dirt path over there at the end of the trees. It must go somewhere. Keep running until you find someone you think will help us. Tell them to call nine-one-one. Just say to them we need help, someone is trapped in the woods." Sandy turned away from Sarah and stood for a minute to gather her thoughts.

Sarah took off running, but she turned around to look back. Sandy saw her and yelled, "Don't look back. Keep going, no matter what happens!"

The brush was wet from last night's rain as Sandy began to run herself. Her clothes were getting soaked. She tripped and fell but got up and ran some more. She could hear voices close behind her and reflections of flashlights against the trees. She ran and then tripped again over weeds and logs. As she stood back up from falling she felt a hand on her back. Something hard hit her head; there was a searing pain in her hip, then nothing but darkness.

Sandy slowly opened her eyes. She couldn't remember a time she had felt so weak and exhausted. She tried to recall what had happened. Vaguely she remembered running in wet clothes through the woods, falling many times, getting back up and running some more. Her hip was painful and beginning to throb like a toothache. Her head hurt. Suddenly, she realized she was up high in the air and something was around her neck. Her feet felt cold as if she was standing on some type of metal. Her hands were tied down against her sides, but she could reach her hip with her fingers.

As she rubbed her hip, a muffled voice said, "Those tranquilizer darts hurt a bit, don't they? We use them on deer."

Sandy looked up and could see all the hooded figures in the faint light coming through the cracks in the shed's wooden slats. They were all swaying in unison and humming or maybe that was just the buzzing in her head. She saw a single figure walk toward the shed door with a gold book held high in their hand. When she heard the voice, she knew it was him.

The Father began to read louder and louder as he reached the shed and kicked the door open. He didn't even pause and with one swift kick, the metal ladder beneath her was gone. Sandy's last thoughts were of Sarah and Carrie and then she saw her Mom's figure in a flash of light as she felt the noose tighten around her neck.

CHAPTER 1

Three months earlier …

Sandy woke to the sound of light rain falling. She stretched and enjoyed the relaxed feeling of knowing she didn't have to go to work. She stood up to look out the window and was surprised to see a police car and ambulance outside in the parking lot. She thought to herself that they were probably there for some elderly tourist who had chest pain or heat exhaustion from the one-hundred-degree heat. On the afternoon she arrived, she was amazed at the evening warmth in South Carolina compared to the night cool she had left in Colorado.

She was about to turn from the window when she saw a stretcher coming out with someone on it. The window was fogged from her air-conditioning hitting the panes, and the light rain coming down made it hard to see out. She caught a glimpse of red hair and realized it looked like the young woman she had seen in the hotel lounge the first night she arrived. She was surprised. That woman was young, probably about twenty-five years old. Maybe she was sick or had an accident.

1

Rummaging for something to put on, she grabbed the jeans and T-shirt she had worn the night before. Just as she headed out the door, the ambulance was driving away. The police were still talking to a group of people next door when she approached them.

"What happened?" she asked. One officer turned around at the sound of her voice.

"Who are you? Did you know the woman staying in this room?" He pointed toward room 119.

"Not really. I saw her the first night I got here. She was leaving her room as I was coming in. Later that night I saw her in the bar. Did something happen to her?"

The officer didn't answer her question but instead asked her, "Did she say anything to you at all?"

"No. I sat down a couple seats over from her and said hello, but she was busy talking to the bartender."

"Did you happen to overhear any of their conversation?" he asked.

"A little bit. I overheard her tell the bartender she was from North Carolina. I remember she was saying something about how she was supposed to meet someone here. What happened to her?" Sandy asked again.

The cop looked at her as he was writing. "Did she say where she was meeting this person?"

"I think I heard her say she was meeting someone at The Beach Grill or someplace like that. As I said, she didn't talk to me. I didn't overhear everything she was saying. It's a small place, but she lowered her voice when she looked over and noticed that I was looking right at them. It was around eight o'clock at night and I was tired. I had one beer and then came back to the room. I wanted to hit the beach early in the morning. She was still there when I left."

"Did you happen to catch her name?" the officer asked.

"I think I heard him call her Karen … maybe. I'm not sure."

"And what's your name?"

"Sandy Milford."

"And do you have some type of ID?" he asked.

"It's in my room."

"Would you please go get it? I have just a few more things to write down, and then I have to go to the morgue."

Sandy sucked in her breath. "She's dead?"

"Yes." He stopped writing and looked intently at her. "Would you please get your ID for me?"

Sandy went back to her room and grabbed her pocketbook. She was heading out the door when she ran into the officer coming toward her.

"Ms. Milford is it?" he asked. "I just wanted to ask you a few more questions without a crowd around. When you noticed this young woman, did she seem to be acting odd at all?"

"No. She seemed fine," Sandy said. "Why?"

"Not one thing in particular. I'm just trying to gather information." The officer was looking down at her driver's license while he was talking to her.

"Did you hear her say anything else at all, Ms. Milford?"

"No." Sandy shook her head. "That's all I remember."

"Thanks. How long will you be staying?" the officer asked.

"I'll be here about two weeks," Sandy answered.

"If you do think of anything else, please give me a call." The officer handed her his card. She read the name on the card: Detective Samuel Carey.

"How did she die?" Sandy asked.

"We're continuing to look into exactly what happened. It appears she may have hung herself. We have to wait until the body is examined. Thanks for the information." Detective Carey put the pad back in his pocket.

Sandy just stood there with her mouth open. She shivered, nodded toward the detective, and went back into her room.

Detective Carey walked back to his partner standing at the car. "So, Chuck, what do you think?"

"It seems odd to me," Chuck replied. "This young woman checked in for two nights. At the desk, they said she paid cash and listed an address in North Carolina. The desk clerk gave me the address she wrote down. There isn't a car here next to her room. The desk clerk said she had a car. There's no ID in her room and we found a purse full of only makeup, mints, gum, and some small change. It doesn't figure. Almost all tourists carry credit cards and at least some spending money in case of an emergency. She barely had enough to buy a couple of sodas."

Detective Carey pulled the pad back out of his pocket. "According to the woman I just spoke with in room one seventeen, our victim was in the bar three nights ago chatting up the bartender. No one recalls seeing her all day yesterday or last night, but the desk clerk reported she called for towels at midnight, and then sometime after that, she must have hung herself. What was she doing for the last two nights?"

Chuck shook his head and looked down at the notes Detective Carey handed him. "This is a strange business, Sam." Chuck started to jot down the dates and times the victim was reportedly seen. "I think we need to establish a good timeline from the night she checked in until now. Since no one remembers seeing her here for the last twenty-four hours, maybe she was somewhere else. I'm going to check all the businesses nearby and see if anyone fitting her description came in recently."

"If we can take a decent picture down at the morgue, I'll see if our department sketch artist at the station can do up a composite drawing of her," Detective Carey said. "The only thing we do know for sure at this point is that the manager said she called for extra towels last night at midnight and he told her the maid would deliver them this morning. Let's assume she was alive at midnight. The maid got there about seven thirty this morning, knocked and when no answered she went in and found her. She started screaming her head off and then called the manager. So where was she up until midnight?" Detective Carey was rubbing his chin.

"The three guys in the room right next door said they didn't hear anything at all until the maid was screaming. They have been here all week, but they were pretty soused most nights. They've been partying down on the beach. Two of the men don't even remember seeing her when they were coming and going to their room. One of the other guys said he thought he remembered seeing her carrying in a grocery bag yesterday or maybe the day before. He couldn't be sure."

"The guy and two girls one room over past the staircase still reeked of alcohol when I was talking to them," Chuck replied. "I'm not sure if they've sobered up yet. I didn't see any groceries in the victim's room and the only other thing in there was a suitcase with enough clothes for about two days. The clothes were all jumbled up like they had been rifled through. There wasn't a bathing suit with the clothes, which seems weird for someone coming to the beach and just one pair of dress shoes. Nothing I would usually expect for a beach vacation." Detective Carey was nodding his head in agreement with what Chuck was saying.

"What about that woman you were just talking to?" Chuck nodded his head in the direction of Sandy's room. "Any chance she is involved?"

"No," Detective Carey replied. "She's just another tourist here on vacation from Colorado. She did seem a little jumpy or nervous about something." He shrugged his shoulders. "Let's go, Chuck. We need to find out everything we can about this young woman and if she has any other connections here. I also need to track down the bartender for this place. Maybe he can fit some pieces into the puzzle." They turned and headed back toward the manager's office at the motel.

Sandy plopped down on her bed. The rain had stopped and now the sun was completely out. She shivered again. She didn't feel like hanging around in her room anymore. She headed to the shower and decided she would go out and hit the stores to find a new bathing suit before going to the beach.

Sandy found two cute bikinis at one of the boulevard beach shops. She was amazed at the number of T-shirt and beachwear shops. There was one at least every two blocks, and some were even two stories high. She went into one that had dozens of different types of shirts, seashells, bathing suits, and multiple kinds of touristy type stuff.

There were tons of restaurants, each with a sign out front proclaiming the best seafood on the beach. She stopped in one close to the boulevard for an early lunch. She ordered the shrimp basket, which included some hushpuppies, a specialty for the area. They turned out to be small balls of cornmeal with a little sweet taste. The waitress told her they were cooked in piping hot oil and every southerner had their own recipe. The shrimp basket also contained coleslaw and French fries. She normally did not eat fried food, but it all was really good.

Sandy spent the rest of the day on the beach, talked to a couple of lifeguards, and ate a light snack at the grill on the pier. It was about five thirty when she got back to the motel. On the beach, she had met a group of girls who said the Sand and Sip Bar was the place to go at night. They all said it had good music and lots of tropical drinks. Plus, it was right on the beach. Sandy felt like a night out. There were loads of bars right on the beach and the warm breezes along with a nice cold beer sounded like it would be just what she needed.

This whole trip had stemmed from a fight with Tom. They had been dating two years and last week he had told her that he might take a job down here in South Carolina. Sandy sat there waiting for him to ask her, "Do you want to go with me?" She expected him to ask even though she had told him she wasn't ready for marriage just two months ago, the thought of his leaving made her sick to her stomach. Tom had told her he loved her and would come back once a month to see her or she could come to visit. He had continued the conversation and said to her he knew how hard she had worked to get her supervisor job at the bank. He also said that he was proud of her as she was making a decent salary considering her bachelor's degree in business. He also brought up the fact that she had lived in Colorado her whole life. Sandy had just sat there tightlipped the whole time he was talking.

She and Tom had always taken vacations to Florida and California because Sandy thought those were the best beaches in the world. She loved lying around in the sun while reading books and just relaxing. South Carolina had never even crossed her mind as a place she might end up living.

When Tom finished talking, Sandy had been so shocked by his announcement about leaving that when he asked where she wanted to go after dinner, she said home. He had tried to get her to talk, but she just couldn't … or wouldn't, as he said. Tom had told her he would call her Saturday morning. Sandy called an airline that very night when she got home and booked a flight to South Carolina. If he was going to be in South Carolina, then she was going to find out about it herself. She was upset and really mad at the same time. How could he just spring something like that on her? She was only able to book a flight into Charleston, South Carolina, so she decided she would rent a car at the airport there and drive to Myrtle Beach. It all had happened so fast and once she was on the road to Myrtle Beach there was no turning back. She had checked into one of the first motels she saw with a vacancy sign. Now, here she was and feeling lonely and a little down. She missed Tom terribly and it was probably wrong of her to leave, but she wanted to make up her own mind about South Carolina. Maybe she would call Tom later tonight. She knew if her Dad were alive he would be fussing at her about her mule headed stubborn streak, as he called it. "Worse than a mule, you are Sandy," he would say and then shake his head. "At least a mule knows when to come back to the barn." As a little girl she would run down to the fields and hide out until dark when she was mad at her brother or her parents. They would all be out calling her name and she would not answer, not even when they yelled supper was ready. Thinking of her Dad made her smile.

As Sandy showered she thought she heard a knock on her door, but when she came out of the shower, she looked out the window and no one was around. She put on one of the summer dresses she had brought with her and pulled her long blonde hair back. She decided not to wear any makeup. She put on her new sandals, which they called flip-flops here in South Carolina and headed out. She drove down toward the boulevard right on the ocean.

When Sandy got back at midnight, she was just a little tipsy. She'd had three drinks, which was over her limit to drive, but then she drank some water and coffee, and decided that since it was only five blocks, she would be okay.

She undressed and went to hang up her clothes. As she hung up her dress she noticed all her clothes were hanging on a different side of the closet or was she just imagining that. She must be tipsier than she thought.

Sandy slept until nine o'clock the next morning. It was Wednesday and she thought that maybe she would just hang around the motel. It had a small restaurant and a pool. After thinking about it a while, she decided to call Tom.

Just as she reached for her room phone, it rang. She picked up the receiver.

"Hello! Ms. Milford, this is Officer Carey. Sorry to call so early, but I just wanted to ask you one more question. Did you happen to notice if the young woman, Karen, had a dog with her? Or did you hear a dog barking at all from your room?"

"No. I don't think they allow pets here. I saw a sign. Why?"

"Just a follow-up question for the investigation," Detective Carey replied.

Forensics had called him that morning with a report that they analyzed some of the specimens from the deceased's room and they had turned out to be canine hairs. Detective Carey had considered that it was possible that some guests prior to the victim could have smuggled a pet in during their stay. However, forensics said they were fresh, not like old dead hairs that come off when a dog sheds. If the motel staff really cleaned rooms between renting, then there should not be fresh dog hairs in the room. He had also seen the NO PETS ALLOWED sign in the office when he was talking to the manager at the desk.

Sandy interrupted his thoughts by asking, "Did you find her family?"

"Yes. We located them and they're coming down," he answered.

"I feel so bad for them," Sandy said. "What a horrible thing."

"You sure she wasn't acting strange when you saw her the other night? Like she was on something?" he asked.

"No. She might have been a little tipsy. She was talking so low, slurred her words maybe a little, but I just figured she had a few too many. The bartender gave her at least two mixed drinks of some kind while I was there."

"Well, her family is coming here on Saturday. If they ask, would you be willing to talk to them?" Detective Carey asked.

"Yes. I guess so. I don't know what I would say to them."

"You were one of the last people to see her, so it might make them feel better. We may need you to come down and give a statement at the police station. We'll be in touch."

"Wait," Sandy said. "Did she have a dog?" Sandy had wondered why he was asking about a dog.

"I asked her family about that. She didn't have a dog or a cat or any kind of pet. One of her daughters had bad allergies. Well, thanks again, Ms. Milford. We'll be in touch."

Sandy felt a pain in the pit of her stomach. That poor woman had children. It was so very sad.

Detective Carey returned to reading the report on his desk. His office had run the dead woman's fingerprints and found she had a record from way back when she was a teenager. She had passed some bad checks. They pulled up the address and phone number associated with the arrest record and called it. It turned out that her parents still lived at that phone number. Notifying family was the part of the job Detective Carey hated the most. He usually tried to involve that city's local law enforcement to go over and notify families, but her parents were so insistent when he called that he broke the news to them. He felt their anguish right through the phone, heard the sobbing as the woman called for her husband. He held on for a few minutes before he asked if they were willing to answer some questions.

Her parents had told Detective Carey that they thought she was at home in Charlotte up until Sunday, when they returned from a trip. They had gone over to her house to drop off some souvenirs for the kids and the family car wasn't there. They'd called and couldn't reach her on her cell phone, which worried them. They said that she was happily married, with two kids, and they had just talked to her five days ago while they were on their trip. That was when Detective Carey had learned about the two girls. She had two daughters that were supposed to be with her. His heart had sunk with the knowledge that there were now two little girls missing also. Her parents told him her husband was a truck driver, so they had called him when they could not reach her. He thought she was at home also. He had spoken to his wife on her cell on Sunday morning, and she didn't say anything was wrong. He said he didn't talk to the girls, as his wife said they were still sleeping. Her parents had also called all her friends and the hospitals then reported her and the girls missing on Monday.

The husband was headed back to North Carolina and he told Detective Carey the same thing her parents had told him. She and the girls were supposed to go to a dance competition in Charleston and return home on Sunday afternoon. They didn't know anything about her going to Myrtle Beach, as she had no friends there and they always took family vacations to the lake. They could not understand why she would have decided to travel to Myrtle Beach.

Detective Carey had told them that the preliminary autopsy showed she had died from asphyxiation. Sedatives were found in her bloodstream. Ativan was the drug detected in her blood analysis, and his partner had found a prescription bottle of Ativan in her room. Her parents said she took them occasionally for nerves. Her parents and husband both said she had never been depressed, was happy, and loved her little girls. She was a Girl Scout leader and a treasurer for the PTA at school, and she was very active in the church. She was always taking her girls to dance competitions in nearby cities. The girls had won several awards and cash prizes. Her family insisted that there was no way she would take her own life. She lived for her family and those two girls.

Detective Carey and his partner had located the bartender, Michael Jones. He worked three nights a week at the Eastside Inn and then was a waiter three days a week at a restaurant in Murrell's Inlet. He said he served the young woman a couple of drinks. She was telling him all about her daughters, saying that she had met an agent who wanted to use her daughters in a commercial for a movie they were making in Myrtle Beach. She was supposed to meet the agent at a restaurant. She was waiting on a call from him. The bartender said she seemed a little tipsy, but not drunk.

That was all he knew. Detective Carey had checked with his other employer, and he was at work at all the times he indicated in his statement. He had no prior arrests. He also had a steady girlfriend. She was his alibi for the last three evenings. Detective Carey felt he was clean as far as being involved. Just one more dead end in this case.

After Sandy had hung up from talking with Detective Carey, she racked her brains wondering if there was something she'd missed? She considered herself very observant. That was one of the reasons she had been promoted at work. Two men had robbed the bank where she was a teller. She had remained calm, giving them the money while they were waving guns around. She had noticed the tattoos on one guy's arm and a scar on the hand of the other guy. They had worn masks, but she noticed that one man had a ring through his eyebrow that was partially showing through the ski mask. When she had given the police descriptions of the two men, they had tracked them down through mug shots. She also had picked them out of the lineup and the money was recovered.

She decided right then that she wanted to talk to Tom. She felt so alone. When Tom answered the phone, she could hear the tiredness in his voice.

"Sandy, where are you? I've been going nuts here. Are you all right?"

"Yes. I'm just a little scared." That was the first time she admitted that to herself.

"Scared? Why?" he asked.

Sandy told him what had happened.

"God, I have been worried sick about you. How could you do this? I love you. I'm coming down there now."

Sandy felt like saying yes, come now, but she knew he had a big conference at his firm this week.

"No, Tom. I'm so sorry. I just had to get away and think about your move, and then I ended up here in South Carolina."

"Sandy, we need to talk. I never meant to spring it on you like that. I was looking at a way to get more financially stable. We talked about having a place together with lots of yard and plenty of space. I thought if I could work the new job for a couple of years, then maybe we would have that chance. I do want a future with you. You're such a loner at times and so independent. I know you've been independent since you were sixteen, but I want to be there for you. I don't want us to be apart. How long are you going to be down there?"

"I took two weeks of vacation. I have five weeks and I just did it impulsively. I know I was wrong. I'm so sorry, Tom. I do love you and I'm happy you got a job where you can make a lot more money. I just never thought about you leaving, and I, well, I just can't imagine being without you either." Tears had started to well up in her eyes.

"I can't live without you either, Sandy. I have this conference today and tomorrow, but I can take some time off after that. Why don't I fly down there on Saturday and we can talk about it?"

"I'd like that. We could be beachcombers for a while." Sandy was starting to feel a little better. Just hearing his voice made her calmer.

"Where are you staying?" Tom asked.

"I'm at the Eastside Inn on the main highway from Charleston, just outside Myrtle Beach," Sandy answered.

"Boy, what a nice name for such a spooky place. We'll stay somewhere else when I get there," Tom said.

Sandy noted the teasing tone in his voice. "What do you mean by spooky?"

"I'm kidding, but I guess that's morbid considering what happened. Sorry! You know, it's weird, that girl hanging herself. Don't you think that it's sort of like murder mystery stuff?" he asked. Tom knew Sandy loved watching the PBS Channel for the old English murder mystery theater. She watched all the new ones and the reruns. He was hoping that might ease the tension he heard in her voice.

"Yes, I guess so. It's such a pretty place. I just never thought of a place like this being spooky. Now an English castle is an entirely different story!" Sandy did laugh aloud then. "Everyone seems nice and normal here."

Then she felt bad for laughing. It truly was a tragedy, real life and not fiction.

"All right, I'll see you on Saturday. What room are you in staying in and what's the phone number there?" Tom asked.

"I'm in room one seventeen. The phone number is faded out on the phone. Just call my cell."

"Okay. See you on Saturday. I love you, Sandy."

"I love you too, Tom, and I miss you."

Sandy suddenly felt better after she hung up. She knew Tom loved her and they could work things out. They had not had a vacation together since last year, when they had gone to a bed-and-breakfast in New England.

This would be a nice change. With the warm weather, tropical breezes, and a beach, it was like being in a small slice of paradise. Sandy could not wait until he got there.

As Tom hung up the phone, he looked over at the box on the nightstand. It held the engagement ring he had planned to give Sandy the other night, but things had just gone all wrong. He knew he hadn't started the conversation out right, just telling her he was going. His investment company had sprung this opportunity on him at work unexpectedly, and when they offered him so much more money, he thought this would be his chance to have that nice big house with a big yard for kids and a garden, as Sandy had always wanted and talked about. It would be so much better than the apartments they both lived in now. The other bonus would be moving to the state where his mother had grown up; maybe he could learn something about her life and her family.

Tom started rummaging in his closet for clothes to pack and then went back to the computer to start booking his flight. He worked from home a lot. He conducted many video conferences with clients, so it gave him a few minutes to get stuff done before the next live chat.

Sandy decided she would go down to the little restaurant to eat and then lay out by the pool. She was hungry now and in a much better mood. She walked by the manager's office on the way to the restaurant. The restaurant and bar were in the building adjacent to the office. She noticed that there appeared to be some more rooms on the second floor above the office. Maybe they were living quarters. As she walked by the office, she saw a cute little brown dog at the glass door and figured it must belong to the owners. The dog didn't even bark; it just stared. She smiled and waved, the dog backed up, and then she glanced up to see an elderly woman standing behind the dog. The woman turned around and the dog followed. Sandy thought to herself that she must be the owner of the motel since she had seen what looked like living quarters behind the desk when she checked in.

Sandy ate a huge meal. She was so full she thought she might not fit into that new bikini when she went to the pool. When she got to the pool, she noticed there was a garden area with palm trees and two hammocks tied to a couple of pine trees. There were picnic tables and a couple of old cabanas. A slight warm breeze was blowing and she decided she would lie in one of the hammocks for a while.

She had noticed that there were not as many cars in the parking lot today as yesterday, but many people probably checked out during the week. Rates were cheaper during the week and went up on weekends. She wondered if any people had checked out due to that poor woman. She tried not to think about it and just let her mind go blank and think about Tom.

The hammock was swinging and she began to doze. She couldn't believe how relaxed she felt. Just as she began to feel her eyes too heavy to open, she thought she heard someone humming.

CHAPTER 2

Tom got to the airport two hours early on Saturday with the ring box in his pocket. He couldn't wait until he saw Sandy. He could visualize her blonde hair, slightly across her left eye, her beautiful blue eyes and the way she tilted her head to the left when she laughed. He couldn't bear the thought of losing her. He hoped she would say yes. He felt good about it after talking to her.

Two months ago, before she had gotten her supervisor position, when they talked about moving in together, she had made it clear she didn't want to get married or depend on anyone else until she knew she could make it on her own. He knew that came from her upbringing. She had been raised on a farm outside of Hot Springs, Colorado. She had worked hard to go to college. She worked two jobs. Her mother had died six years ago from a heart attack and her father two months later from a broken heart, which is what Sandy believed. Her Dad just sat home and would not go out and work in the fields anymore. Her parents had been married fifty years.

Sandy had one brother, who had carried on the farm business. They grew feed for cattle and horses and also grew their own vegetables. Tom had visited with her once, and he had loved it. Her brother was the strong and silent type, and his wife was an itty-bitty thing. They had five children, worked in the fields, and managed to cook a big dinner every night. They had two hundred acres, and Tom understood why Sandy wanted a big house with a big yard.

Tom and Sandy had met at his office building by chance. Sandy was attending night classes at a nearby business college. His company had offered use of computer workrooms at night for qualifying scholarship students at the school. Quite often they would end up recruiting some of the students to work at his firm.

Working late one night, he had walked by the workroom and seen her sitting at one of the tables. She had such long blonde hair and lanky legs. He had run into the doorframe looking at her.

It took him three night of working late before he walked in and sat down next to her and asked her out. He knew it was love at first sight, whether she did or not. It had taken five dates just to get her to give him a long kiss good night. He smiled when he thought about her and that kiss. She had such soft kissable lips, and when he looked in her eyes, such a feeling of warmth came over him. No one had ever had that effect on him except for his mom. The feeling was if everything was right in the world and nothing else mattered.

The speaker announced his plane boarding and he headed toward the gate.

CHAPTER 3

When Sandy opened her eyes it was very dark. She faintly remembered falling asleep, but was it night already? She rolled over and then realized she was on the floor. She tried to stand up, but her eyes had not adjusted to the light and she felt woozy. She took a step and almost stumbled. She couldn't figure out where she was. What time was it?

She heard some movement behind her, and she jumped and turned. "Who's there?"

"Be quiet," she heard what sounded like a child's voice say. "They'll hear you."

"Who will hear me?" Sandy asked.

"Father's disciples," the voice answered.

Sandy headed toward where the voice was coming from, and she could see a little light filtering in from somewhere. At first, it appeared as if she was in a basement or something. In the faint light, she saw two small figures sitting on the edge of what looked like a steel bed. The figures were two little girls wearing white dresses. The dresses were not fancy. They were plain with no ribbons or bows.

"Who are you?" Sandy asked.

"I'm Sarah, and this is Rebecca," the one on the left said. Rebecca looked up at Sandy. "Do you know where my mommy is?"

Sandy just stood and stared at the two little girls. Rebecca started to sniffle, and Sarah put her arms around her.

"Where are we, Sarah?" Sandy asked.

"Shh! He'll hear you."

"Who will hear me, Sarah?" Sandy was standing in front of her then.

"The father," Sarah answered.

"What father? I don't understand. Do you mean your father?" Sandy leaned over toward her.

"The man who brought us here told us the man in the robe is the father. He said the father took our mommy away because we cried. Do you know where our mommy is?" Both of the little girls were looking up at her.

Sandy sat down hard on the floor. Oh God. Where was she? She still felt a little weak and woozy. She tried to get her head clear. She looked down and realized she was wearing a long plain white gown.

"No, Sarah, I don't know where your Mommy is." Sandy felt tears in her eyes, and then that determination she had had her whole life took over. She would not give in and feel sorry for herself. She had to think. She knew without a doubt that she was in big trouble.

CHAPTER 4

Tom landed at the airport in Charleston on Saturday afternoon. He had to catch a short flight from there to Myrtle Beach. He had an hour delay, so he decided to call Sandy. He called her cell and the phone rang, but there was no answer and it did not go to voicemail. Maybe her voicemail was full or off. The phone just buzzed after a few rings. Maybe there was no reception if she was out on the beach. He had left a message at the front desk for her to call him back, but the guy on the phone didn't seem too interested or too bright. Oh well. He would be there soon.

While he was waiting for the plane, he noticed a petite brunette walking up to the desk to speak to a flight attendant. She carried a backpack and had on no makeup, but her skin seemed to glow with health. When she turned around and caught him looking, she smiled, and he noticed that she had bright green eyes and a beautiful smile. Her smile reminded him of Sandy's smile and he smiled back.

The plane left Charleston at seven that night. The plane was a small one with only twenty seats. It was only a short flight, so he didn't mind. He was seated behind the nice-looking brunette girl. He closed his eyes and began nodding off. He wanted to be refreshed and wide-awake when he saw Sandy.

He woke up and heard the flight attendant telling the girl she was so sorry about her sister and how awful that must be for her family. He tuned in to listen.

"My family and I go to Myrtle Beach every summer," he heard the flight attendant saying. "We just love it. I'm so sorry that it will be a sad place for you."

"Thank you," the woman replied. "I still can't believe she's gone. We just hope we can find our nieces." The attendant nodded her head, patted the ladies shoulder and walked off.

Tom leaned forward. "Excuse me. I don't mean to eavesdrop, but I heard you say something about your sister." He didn't know if he should ask or not, but something compelled him to do so. "My girlfriend is staying in Myrtle Beach, and there was a woman who died at the motel, Eastside Inn, where she's staying. Was that your sister?"

"Yes, that was Karen," she was choking back tears as she talked. "Who's your girlfriend?"

"Sandy Milford." He noticed the woman's brows wrinkle, and she looked puzzled. "Sandy's the name of the woman we were supposed to talk to when we got there. The detective gave us her name. Do you know where she is?"

"Yes. As I said, she's staying right there at the same motel."

She was looking at him strangely. "What's your name?" she asked.

"Tom Barton."

"Well, Tom, the detective told us that he tried to reach her to let her know that my brother-in-law and I would be there today, and the person at the motel said she checked out Thursday night. No one has seen her. She didn't say where she was going. Have you talked to her?" The brunette had a questioning look on her face.

Tom was starting to get a sick feeling in his stomach.

"No. I talked to her Wednesday and told her I was coming. I was supposed to meet her there. I don't understand what's going on. She wouldn't just leave. We were going to spend the rest of the weekend together. I haven't been able to reach her, but I figured she was out on the beach. I called the office and left a message for her to call me and they didn't tell me she had checked out."

"Tom, my name's Liz Thomas." Her voice had softened. "Maybe it was just a misunderstanding. Maybe she left a note for you. We'll find out when we get there. I talked to my brother-in-law. He's still there at the motel. There hasn't been any news or leads yet about my sisters' daughters either. All we want is to find them unharmed. I'm sure everything is okay with your girlfriend." She gave him a smile and then turned back forward as the announcement came on that they were landing in a few minutes.

Tom pulled out his cell phone to try the number again, but then he noticed the seat belt light come on. He would have to wait.

When they landed, he immediately turned his phone on. There were no messages on his phone. He called his voicemail at his home; nothing from Sandy. He just wanted to get off the plane and get to that motel. He was racking his brains for an answer when Liz turned around again. "Tom, is someone meeting you at the airport?"

"No, I've arranged for a rental car."

"Well, my brother-in-law is picking me up. Would you like a ride to the motel? We would be glad to give you a ride."

"No thanks. I believe I would like my own wheels. That way I can find Sandy." Tom was already up grabbing his bag out of the overhead bin.

Liz had a worried look in her eyes. "I hope everything is all right. I'm sure it will be." She stood up and started getting her belongings together.

The pilot announced that they would be deplaning in a few minutes.

Tom opened his briefcase and pulled out his recorder. He had to sort this all out. Maybe if he recorded some notes, it might help. Tom used his recorder a lot for work. He planned many programs like that and set his schedule, thinking about dates and times and saying them aloud into the recorder. Sandy would have been missing … He stopped and thought about that word: _missing_! Sandy would have been missing two days as of today. He knew in his heart that Sandy wouldn't have just run off, not again!

He didn't understand why he was even thinking that she was missing. But, this whole situation was just getting weirder by the minute and he had a feeling that something was very wrong.

CHAPTER 5

Sandy was working her way around the building she was in. She was trying to see if there was any way out and what was on the outside. The last two days had been somewhat blurry. She had not eaten any of the food that had been set out on the table since yesterday. She had been sleeping so much that she had decided the food must be drugged.

She spent most of her time with Rebecca and Sarah. There were two older girls in the building with them. Lila and Mary were their names. She had a hard time getting them to talk to her. They were quiet and looked furtively around when they did speak, as if they were afraid someone was listening. She did get Lila and Mary to tell her they had been camping out when they met two nice young boys who invited them to a party. They both were sixteen years old, and when Sandy asked why they were on their own, they admitted they had run away from home and were backpacking and camping here and there. When they went to the party with the boys, at least thirty people were there. They said that it was more like a church service. The next thing they knew, they had woken up in here. There had been no one else here when they arrived about two weeks ago.

Sarah and Rebecca had come about a few days ago. They had already told Sandy they had woken up in another place with their mommy. Their mom had yelled and banged on the walls and then two men had come and taken her away. Sandy continued to ask them more questions trying to figure out how they got here. They told Sandy their mom had met a man and a woman at the dance recital. The man told their mom that they wanted to have the girls be in a dance movie at the beach. Their mother told them it would mean lots of money and that they would surprise Daddy with it when he got home. Sarah and Rebecca said they had never been to Myrtle Beach. Their mom had promised them they could go play on the beach some after they got there. Sarah said they had gone to sleep one night and woken up with their mom in jail. Sandy thought they must be mistaken, but Sarah had said it had bars and beds just like the jail on TV in *Law and Order.* Their Mommy watched that show in the afternoons when they got home from school. She let them watch it sometimes, but most of the time she sent them to their room to play.

The bad man took them out of the jail and put them in a big van and brought here. He told them if they didn't be quite, they would never see their Mommy again.

Sandy was amazed at how brave they were being. She sat with them and had pulled her cot over to sleep close to them since the first night. She could not believe it when they told her they were only six and eight years old.

Sandy could see through some of the cracks in the wooden part of the building. Not far away she saw some barns, a couple of houses and fields off in the distance. The building they were in looked like an old warehouse or storage place. The ceilings were about thirty feet high and had some skylights. There were old grimy-looking panes of glass that let some light in at night and even more when the sun came up. There were no light switches that she could find, but two old metal lights high up on the wall went on and off sometimes at night. She decided they must control them on the outside.

There was a big double sink at the end of the room with some towels and washcloths. There was also a stack of white gowns, sort of like the kind Sandy had seen the members of the choir wear when she was a child. Sandy had helped the children wash up and take off their dresses the second night she was there, and put one of the small gowns on each of them. They had all eaten some of the fruit and bread left for them. There were no plates only paper towels. The only other thing on the table was copies of a book with a bright gold cover. She had picked up a copy to read, as the girls had asked her to read aloud to them last night. The title of the book was *The Book of Truth.* Inside, the pages were typed, not professionally but as if on an old electric typewriter. Some of the book had Bible verses, but mostly it was the story of how God spoke to Ezra and guided Ezra through visions as to how God wanted all his followers to live. It was evident to Sandy that all women must be subservient to the man called the father and be clean, pure and work the land. As Sandy read, the girls clung to her and cried quietly. She tried her best to calm them down. She had decided to read from the section titled "God's Plan for All Children," but she noticed right away that the verses seemed to be rambling and the punctuation was wrong. Some of the chapters in the book were "The Story of Kane," "The Story of Miss Mary," and "The Life of Sarah. "She noticed that the wording was different, with a lot of old language and strange phrases. They seemed more like short stories. She found a couple of stories that she thought were okay to read to the girls, but there was a lot about Ezra being the servant of God who spoke for God, and all who followed Ezra would be rewarded by riches, salvation, and cleansed of all their sins. She left out many parts of the stories and ad-libbed others. She would not allow the girls to have a book to read by themselves.

Lila and Mary read every night. During the day, they were let out by a man who shoved Sandy back when she came toward the steel door. They both came back at night. When Sandy tried to talk to them, they told her the father said they could not talk to her anymore and that she needed to be quiet. They began to keep to themselves and stayed on the other side of the shed. She noticed their books that they read each night had their names written on the front of them. They had become even less interactive and quieter.

Last night Sandy had woken up in the middle of the night and the girls were gone. She looked all around, even down in the corner where there was a makeshift toilet. There was a small closet-like area at the end of the room, next to the big steel door, and there was a single toilet. There was no mirror, no sink, and the toilet had rust stains, but it flushed. There was a door to the toilet, but no handle and no lock. Still, it was the one place Sandy felt she had some peace and privacy.

Later that night, Sandy heard the door open and the girls come back in. When she heard the other footsteps fade away, she whispered, "Where did you go?"

"To see the father," they answered at the same time.

"Why?" she asked.

"He wants us to be of the light and be saved," they answered in unison.

"We need to hush, Mary," Lila said. "He told us not to talk to her. If we talk, we'll be punished."

"Punished how?" Sandy asked, looking toward Mary. Mary just shook her head no. Lila didn't answer.

"I just want to help you," Sandy said. "Please tell me. We need to try to get out of here."

Then Sandy heard a voice through the door. It was deep and calm, yet something about it was menacing.

"No one leaves the cleansing house until they understand the power of the Divine One. You all must be saved. You can only be saved by reading the book and remaining in silence."

The word "silence" had an emphasis on it, which let Sandy know they needed to be quiet. She noticed that Rebecca and Sarah were awake and shaking. Their eyes were opened real wide. She went over and sat next to them. She hugged them both.

Lila and Mary went to lie down on their cots and did not say another word.

Sandy had a feeling of doom. It was the first time she really thought that they were not going to get out of there. She felt hopeless. Then she thought about Tom. Tom should be here by now. Would he think she had run away again? Would he look for her? Please let him look!

CHAPTER 6

When the plane landed in Myrtle Beach, Tom was the first person off. He went straight to the rental counter. He gave his name and ID.

"What kind of car would you like, Mr. Barton? You asked for an upgrade on your reservation," the clerk handed him his credit card and ID back.

"A truck," he said. He didn't know why he said it, but he just had a feeling he needed something tough. When the clerk had asked for his credit card, Tom thought about the rental car Sandy had. Maybe he could check and see if she'd returned it.

As he was standing at the counter, Liz approached. She had a man and woman with her.

"Tom, this is my brother-in-law, John James, and my mother, Bessie Thomas. He nodded and stuck out his hand to the man. The man looked worn. There were dark circles under his eyes and his face red, as if he had been out in the sun too long.

Liz tells me you're the boyfriend of the woman that saw my wife. She's missing too?" Mr. James was rubbing his forehead as he waited for Tom's answer.

Tom looked at him and saw the look of desperation in his eyes. "Liz told me the desk clerk told you that my girlfriend, Sandy, left the motel. I didn't know anything about it. I talked to her on Wednesday morning and told her I would be down today. I'm going to the motel and then I'm going to talk to the police. I just don't think she would leave like that." He didn't see any point in mentioning the fact that she had run off down here without telling him. "I'll see you at the motel," he said to them both.

"You're welcome to follow us if you like," said Mr. James. "It's right on the main highway that bypasses town."

Tom thanked him and told him he would catch up with them there. He thought he would look around the town and beaches first. He wanted to learn his way around.

Tom picked up the truck at the entrance. It was a new blue Dodge pickup and had all the extras. It was fifty dollars per day, but he felt safe in it. Then he realized that that was an odd thought to have. Why did he need to be safe?

It was nearly two hours later before Tom got to the Eastside Inn. He pulled up to the office and saw an elderly woman staring out the door. By the time he got out of the truck, she was gone. He entered and saw a young man standing behind the desk.

"Good evening, may I help you?" he asked.

"Yes, I'd like to get a room and check on my girlfriend who was staying here."

The man looked closely at him. "What was her name?" he asked.

"Sandy Milford. I heard she checked out and I was supposed to meet her here. When did she check out?" Tom asked.

"The detective already asked about her. Have you talked to the detective?" the clerk asked.

"No. Not yet," Tom answered.

The desk clerk continued. "Well, Ms. Milford checked out late Thursday night. She said she was meeting some friends and was going to stay with them."

"What friends?" Tom asked. "She didn't know anybody here."

The young man shrugged his shoulders. "She didn't say—just said she wanted to check out."

Did she pay with a credit card?" Tom asked.

"No. She paid in cash. You still want a room?" he asked.

"Yes, one close to where Sandy stayed … or is the room she stayed in available?" Tom was staring at the man's face trying to read his expression. The clerk spoke with such a monotone voice, no emotion.

"No. Some woman just rented it," the clerk said. "The room next door is available."

"Alright, I'll take that one." Tom handed him his credit card and noticed that the man just handwrote the number down. When the clerk saw him watching, he said, "Our machine's down. I'll give you a receipt when you check out. How long will you be staying?"

"Seven days for now. Then we will see." Tom took the key and headed to the room. Once inside, he threw his bag on the bed. "Okay, what now?" he asked himself.

He went back out and knocked on the door of 117. No answer.

He decided to walk around the place. He realized he was hungry. He found the restaurant just as it was closing, but they said he could have a burger. He got a burger, ate it quickly, and went to his room.

The motel was set off by itself from the highway. A winding road that ran past it looked as if it went for a distance back down into the woods. There was a chicken barn down the street and a few old houses. He had passed several other motels coming in, like a Holiday Inn and Hampton Inn, and there were quite a few golf courses.

He decided he would look up his Uncle Jake's number. Maybe he could be of some help. Tom had last seen him when he'd come to his mother's funeral. Uncle Jake was his mother's brother, and Tom liked him. The guy had seemed pretty levelheaded. Tom's mother had met and married his father and moved up North and never looked back, or so she had said. Uncle Jake was the only one who ever came to Colorado to visit. He was a widower now. His wife had died from cancer ten years earlier, and he had sent an occasional card to Tom and called Tom's parents once in a while. Since the funeral, Tom had only heard from Uncle Jake twice.

He noticed that most of the license tags in the motel parking lot were from northern states. They were most likely tourist. It was about one a.m. and he was exhausted. He decided he needed to rest and that he would contact his uncle early in the morning. He hoped the number was in the phone book, as he'd forgotten to program it into his cell phone. He had rummaged through his Mom's papers to find it before he left home. Now he couldn't find that scrap of paper.

Tom woke at six o'clock in the morning and looked up Jake Simmons in the phone book. He dialed the number, and a man answered on the second ring.

"Jake Simmons?" Tom asked.

"Yes. Who's this?"

"It's Tom. Tom Barton."

"Tom. I'll be damned. I haven't talked to you in a spell. Where are you?"

"I'm here in Myrtle Beach. I would like to come over and see you today if that's okay."

"Sure boy. Where are you staying?" his uncle asked.

"At the Eastside Inn," Tom answered. Tom noticed that there was a long pause of silence. "You know where it is?" Tom asked.

"Yes. I know," his uncle replied. "You want me to come pick you up?"

"No. I have a rented truck. Give me directions and I'll drive over this morning."

"Why don't you get out of that motel and come over and stay with me?" his uncle said. Tom could have sworn there was an edge to his voice.

"No. It's a long story, but I want to stay here for now." Tom briefly filled him in about what had happened.

He wrote down the directions Jake gave him and hung up.

At seven, there was a knock on his door. Tom was already up and getting dressed. His uncle was standing there.

"I decided to come over here anyway," Jake said. "Tom, I'm really glad to see you. Hard to believe it's been two years. You sure look a lot like your Ma." He reached out and gave him a big hug. "Let's grab some breakfast and talk."

They walked out to the parking lot and to a brand-new truck. He was surprised his uncle had a new truck, as he remembered his mother saying to him how miserly his uncle Jake had always been. His mother always said his uncle never missed a chance to pinch a penny. He was so tight he squeaked when he walked.

"I heard from Grace that you might be moving down to this area," his uncle said.

Grace had been a friend of the family for years, and when she had moved to South Carolina for a job two years earlier, Tom had kept in touch with her, also giving her Uncle Jake's number. She had told Tom when she called that his uncle had come by the real estate office occasionally to say hi.

"So tell me about this job down here," Jake said.

"It's a job on Pawley's Island. I interviewed over video chat and they seem like a great bunch of people. The company offered me a lot more money, and the market is really hot here right now for financial planners."

"So, Tom, what do you want to do?" His uncle was staring at him intently.

"I'm not sure. I thought we would start at the police station and go from there."

"Okay, I'll take you there," Jake said.

They stopped and got a couple of biscuits and coffee on the way.

When they got to the police station and Tom started telling the story, the desk sergeant stopped him and said, "Wait, you need to talk to Detective Carey."

Within a couple of minutes, Detective Carey walked out and shook Tom's hand. "I just met your girlfriend last week. We tried to contact her to come down to the office, and the clerk said she left. We thought that was odd, as she had told me she was staying all week. We couldn't reach her at the phone number she gave us. We've been trying to track her down since then. Are you saying you don't know where she is?"

"Yes, that's right," said Tom. "She called me and told me where she was and what had happened with that other young woman, saying that she was going to stay the rest of the week. I decided to come down here and spend the weekend. We were going to make a brief vacation out of it. Now she is gone and no one has seen her."

Detective Carey was looking at him funny. "So you didn't know she was in Myrtle Beach?"

Tom blushed. "Well, we had a little argument, and then she came here. As he began to explain, he noticed that the detective pulled out a pad and started to write things down.

"Look, Detective Carey, I love her. I know this sounds a little crazy, but if you knew Sandy, you would know that she's very independent; when she makes her mind up to do something, there's no stopping her. You have to help me find her. I have a feeling that something's wrong."

"And who is this?" Detective Carey was staring at Uncle Jake.

"This is my uncle." Tom nodded toward Jake.

His uncle had taken a seat in a chair against the wall. He leaned forward and stuck his hand out. "Howdy, my name is Jake Simmons."

"So, Tom, you have relatives down here?" the detective asked.

"Yes. I haven't met any of them, except Uncle Jake. I had thought that once I came to work down here, I might get to know some of them. My mother was estranged from her family, except for my uncle here. I was offered a job down here and I was talking about moving. I wanted Sandy to come with me after I got settled, but I didn't say that to her. She hadn't agreed to marry me yet. Then we had the fight, and I guess she decided to come see the area for herself. I couldn't believe she had run off like that, and then she called. Please … is there anything that you can tell me? Have you found out anything at all?" There was desperation in Tom's voice.

Detective Carey addressed his comments toward Jake. "Simmons? Are you any relation to the Simmons family who own the funeral home and seafood place by the river?"

"Yes, they're cousins of mine and Tom's."

"I like the food at the River Camp. Good catfish," Detective Carey said. Then he looked back toward Tom.

"Look, Mr. Barton. I'll file a missing person's report, and we have already had someone over there to check out your girlfriend's room. You haven't been in there and touched anything, have you?"

"No, but the clerk told me last night when I checked in that some woman rented it. When I went to the door, there was a DO NOT DISTURB sign on the door. I knocked a couple of times."

"Damn. I told that young man behind the desk not to rent out that room that we might need to come back and look around again. What room did you say you were staying in?"

"I'm in room number one eighteen," Tom said.

"I'll let the detective that comes over there know. He'll probably stop by. We'll do everything we can to help find Ms. Milford. Meanwhile, maybe you better check and make sure she's hasn't turned back up in Colorado." Detective Carey had put the pad down and was looking at something on his desk. "He pushed the pad toward

Tom. "If you don't mind, write down your number so I can reach you if needed."

Tom started writing on the pad and addressed his comments to the Detective.

"I did check to see if Sandy was back in Denver. I called her apartment and office on the way over here this morning, and they haven't seen her or heard from her." Tom shook the detective's hand and got up. He and his uncle walked out.

Detective Carey watched them leave. He was trying to size them up. Tom was well built, clean-cut, dark hair and dark blue eyes. He seemed sincere. Jake Simmons was a different story. He was weather-beaten, had a farmer's tan, was balding, had beefy hands, and looked tough as nails.

Of the two of them, Detective Carey would rather tangle with Tom than his uncle.

"What next?" his uncle asked as they walked out of the station.

"Let's start down at the beach," Tom said. "Sandy ate in some restaurant and bar down there, and maybe someone saw her or she talked to someone. Maybe someone remembers her. Anything that might help figure out where she is or what has happened to her …" Tom began to rub his head. Tom's uncle reached over and patted him on the shoulder.

"Hang in there, son. We won't stop trying until we find her."

Tom looked at him and faintly smiled. He was glad he had someone to go through this with. Yet, he noticed his uncle had a distant look in his eye. He had seen that look in his dad's eyes once when his mom was going through chemo, a long time before she died. She had stage four breast cancer. She lived another two years, but was always weak and sick at the end. Six months after she died, his Dad was killed in a car wreck. Tom had always felt she only did the treatments to stay around for his Dad after she was first diagnosed. They loved each other so much. That look, that same look he had seen in his Dad's eyes, was grief and sadness. He wondered why Uncle Jake had that look. Tom shook it off. No bad thoughts. Tom couldn't let a bad thought creep into his head. Sandy was fine. She must have just gone somewhere else. She would call soon. He just knew it!

CHAPTER 7

Sandy had spent more time recently trying to discover every little detail of the barn, or shed, or whatever it was they were in. It looked as if the one rusted toilet and single pipe makeshift shower head were really old. The plumbing pipes were exposed and looked like they had been haphazardly put together. They were a tangled maze of different kinds of pipes.

There were plenty of bars of soap, towels, shampoo, and toilet tissue. Plus there were new white gowns to wear and sandals left every day when the food was brought. They were told to go to the other end of the shed when the food was delivered. Two big burly men always delivered the food. There were toothbrushes lined up on the sink and disposal coffee cups to rinse with, like the kind you see in restaurants.

She noticed that the big trash can in the middle of the shed where they threw their trash had not been emptied. Surely someone would have to come in sometime and empty it, which might give her a chance to get close to the door. She had to find somehow to get close enough to run out or figure out how to jimmy or pick the door lock. She could see through a crack a slide bolt on the outside. The hinges were new, and the screws on her side had been welded over.

Sandy thought about stopping up the toilet so someone would have to come fix that, and maybe she could get the jump on them. Sandy's thoughts always went back to Rebecca and Sarah. If she got out, should she try to take them or just run and try to find some help? She needed to plan and think this through carefully. Finally, she decided she would bide her time and make sure it was a good plan before she did anything.

Sandy looked over at the little girls huddled on the cots and decided she would try to talk to Lila and Mary again. Surely they must still want out of here. Deep down, Sandy realized that she was the one who must think ahead for all of them.

Sandy wandered around the walls slowly, once again looking for cracks, openings, anything that might mean a way out or boards she could loosen or use for a foothold to get up to the skylights. The skylights looked as if they could be pushed open.

The floor was dirt in some places, with boards in the middle where their cots and the table holding the books were. She noticed that all of the lights were single bulbs hanging down way up on the ceiling. She had now decided they seemed to be on some kind of timer switch or controlled from the outside. Any receptacle or switch she had found inside the building did not seen to work any of the lights.

There were large jugs of water and tea on the tables. Sandy had even thought about using one of them for a weapon to knock the men out. They were plastic, but pretty heavy when they were full.

As she continued to go slowly around the building, she stepped on something rough. She looked down and noticed a concrete slab. It was old and chipped, and next to it was an old rusted metal door covered by dirt. She pulled on it, and it moved a little. Maybe it was an old storm shelter or something. She got down on her knees and started scraping back the dirt around the concrete and metal. Some of the concrete came off in pieces, and she could see a small crack. She tried to look down, but there was only darkness. She was still peering in there when she heard one of the girls calling her name. She stood up and turned around. Mary was standing next to her cot and motioning for her to come over.

She walked back. "What is it, Mary?"

"I think I hear him coming."

"Who's coming?" Sandy looked at her. Then she heard the footsteps.

"The father is coming. It's time for our lesson," Mary whispered.

"What lesson? You haven't said anything about a lesson," Sandy said sternly.

Sandy reached out toward Mary, and Mary backed away.

Then she heard a booming voice from above. "Ours is the way for those who are lost. God said that woman shall come to man, and man shall come to serve the Divine One for all the days."

Sandy looked up and tried to figure out where the voice was coming from. It was dark up in the rafters toward the ceiling.

"Look, you jerk, I don't know who you are and what you want, but you need to let us out of here! You have no right to scare these little girls like this."

"Blasphemy from a sinner!" he shouted back. "You need to be cleansed."

Sandy started to open her mouth again, and then she was hit with a strong cold blast of water, so forceful it knocked her down. The little girls were screaming, and the older girls just crouched down on the floor and began to rock back and forth.

Sandy was cussing and yelling, and then she reached out for the little girls once she could get to her feet. She was soaking wet, and the water stopped.

She heard his voice: "When you repent, the lesson will begin again."

She heard scraping, like a door closing, but she couldn't see anything, and then it was quite again. They were all soaking wet. She hugged the little girls and told them not to cry.

Mary and Lila both stood up, and then Mary said, "You can't talk to him like that. He will make you repent." They both walked off toward the shower.

The food table had been blown over with the water blast, and all of the food was on the floor. She hugged the little girls again and told them to sit very still. Sandy went over and tried to clean up and salvage some of the fruit, bread, and tea, but most of it was soggy. The tea jug had landed straight up, but the water jug had busted.

She heard the shower running at the end of the shed. She yelled out, "Don't use all the hot water! I need to get these girls cleaned up."

When Mary and Lila came back, they just looked at her with blank faces. They looked as if they were sleepwalking.

She gathered up Sarah and Rebecca and took them over and gave them a warm shower, rubbed them dry, and put clean gowns on them. There were no dry shoes for them to wear, so she left them barefoot. They didn't want to let go of her, so she sat them on the floor while she showered. She took them back and then stripped all their cots of wet linens and blankets. Mary and Lila had already gone to bed.

After that, Sandy plopped down in one of the chairs and put her head in her hands. What was she going to do?

Sarah and Rebecca sat at her feet and just stared up at her. She had never felt so helpless in her life. She could see faint filtrations of sunlight streaming in from cracks above, and she could swear she heard movement. Whoever was watching over them, it did not seem to be a divine source.

CHAPTER 8

Tom spent all afternoon going from business to business on the beach, showing people Sandy's picture. He found one bartender in the afternoon who said he had seen her on Monday. He said that she was alone and that she had been a little red, as if she had been in the sun, saying he'd noticed because she had fair skin like most of the people that came down from the North in the summer and always ended up getting sunburned. He asked Tom why he was looking for her.

"She's missing!" Tom replied.

The bartender shook his head. "That's the one thing I don't like about this tourist town. I came to work down here five years ago, and it seems like every year since I have been here, some pretty girl goes missing or is killed. Mostly runaways, people figure, but it never gets any easier when you hear it. I left New York because my brother and his wife were killed in a grocery store robbery, and then you come here and realize that there is grief everywhere you go. You can't escape it, even in a nice friendly town like this. I sure hope you find her, mister!"

Tom thanked him and walked away. His uncle was over by the window, staring out at the street.

"It is a pretty little town, isn't it, Tom?" He didn't wait for an answer before continuing. "Most of the families in this area have been here all their lives, started out as farmers like your relatives and then moved on to other businesses when the tourist started pouring in. Along with the tourists came more crime …" He paused, his head hanging down. "It's not like it used to be—too much wildness, too many sinners." He looked up at Tom, who had approached him, and Tom could have sworn he saw tears in his eyes.

"Let's keep looking," Jake said. He turned and started toward the door.

"I'm ready to go back to the motel for now," Tom said. "We can stop and get something to eat on the way."

Once his uncle dropped him off at the motel, Tom found himself pacing back and forth in the room. He tried to watch the nightly news, but he just couldn't seem to settle down.

Finally, at eleven o'clock, he dozed off for a minute, and then he heard what sounded like some bumping noises coming from the back wall in the bathroom. He got up, walked in the bathroom, and listened. He heard just faint rustling and the bumping noises, but then it was quiet. He shrugged and figured it must be the people next door, and then he remembered that he was in the corner room and the bathroom was on the outside wall.

He went to the door, opened it, and peeped out. He saw two men coming out of the supply closet on the corner; they turned and looked at him, then just turned back around and walked off. They were carrying a couple of boxes.

He thought it a bit late to be doing maintenance, but then he shrugged and went back in. He needed to get some sleep and start again early tomorrow. Tom had told his uncle he would pick him up at six in the morning.

Tom rolled over and looked at the clock. It was 5:45 a.m. He jumped up and headed to the shower. After he showered and shaved, he rushed over to his uncle's house. His uncle was already up and sitting on the porch, a mug in his hand.

"Want some coffee, boy?"

"Yeah, I can sure use it," Tom said.

"Have a seat and I'll get it for you."

He sat down and noticed his uncle had been reading a book. Jake had turned it face down on the small table on the porch. Tom picked it up. *God's Word on the Heathen Tribes* was the title. It was bound in red leather, and no author was listed on the cover.

His uncle returned, and Tom held the book up. "Doing a little light breakfast reading, Uncle Jake?"

His uncle reached for the book and gave him a strained smile. "Yeah, you never know when you might be attacked by a heathen tribe." He gave a little forced laugh and handed Tom the coffee. He walked back into the house with the book. When he came back out, he sat down and looked at Tom.

"Tom, I know how heartbroken you must be over this gal, but do you think there's any chance she met another fella down here and maybe just ran off?"

"No," Tom answered emphatically. "If you knew her, you would know that it's not like her. She is too kind and sweet to do anything like that without at least calling me. I love her, and I know she loves me."

"So, where do you want to start today?" Jake asked him.

"I want to drive to Charleston. Sandy rented a car there at the airport as she could not get a flight all the way into Myrtle Beach. I didn't have enough time between flights to check it out when I was there. So, I want to drive down and see if it's been returned."

"Did you tell the police that?" Uncle Jake asked.

"No. I thought I would follow my own clues. They don't seem to be getting anywhere."

"Fine, Tom. I'll ride with you. Maybe we can stop by Pawley's Island on the way back and I can show you where some of your relatives grew up."

"Okay," Tom said. They got in his rental truck and headed off. Jake made mostly small talk, but he had to ask Tom some things twice before Tom heard him. Tom was thinking repeatedly in his head about the last conversation he'd had with Sandy. Did he miss something or had she really just run off again? He should call Denver again today and make sure no one had heard from her. Maybe she had gone to see her brother. He didn't want to alarm them by calling and asking if she was there, so he was trying to think up an excuse to call. Maybe he could tell them he was about to propose and wanted to know how they felt about that.

He heard Jake say, "Take a right coming up here and get on the interstate to go to the airport."

Tom realized he needed to cross over three lanes, so he gunned the engine and changed over to get to the exit. The truck had quick acceleration and he thanked himself again for choosing a truck.

At the airport, Tom went up to each rental stand with a picture of Sandy he had brought with him and showed it to each clerk. He told each of them the story, and at the fourth counter a clerk said he remembered her, adding that the police had called to check about the car also.

"I told them," The agent said, "that when we got here on Sunday, the keys were in the drop box for the car she rented. We put the balance due on her credit card. The tank was full and she had filled out all of the paperwork in advance. We figured she had to catch an early plane and that is why we have the system worked out like we do."

"Did she leave anything behind in the car?" Tom asked.

"No. We check when they are returned and then the local police came and went over the car for fingerprints and stuff. Unfortunately, it was after the car had already been washed by our guy that does them when they come back in, before we rent them out again. He told them there was red clay on the tires, but other than that, nothing."

"Where is he?" Tom asked.

"Probably at the shed or car wash down at the end of the circle," the clerk replied. He pointed to a large building outside toward the long term parking area.

"Thanks." Tom turned and headed out. His uncle followed. The clerk yelled after them, "Just ask for Danny! That's his name."

Tom found the car wash and walked up to a couple of guys standing around smoking.

"One of you guys named Danny?"

They both turned and looked at him. One guy had dark hair, a pierced nose with a ring, and a lip stud. "Who wants to know?" he asked.

Tom moved closer, and the guy stepped back. "Look, my name is Tom. My girlfriend is missing and the clerk at the counter said one of you guys, Danny, cleaned the car she rented from here. I just wanted to ask a question."

"Oh," the guy said. He relaxed his posture. I just wanted to make sure you ain't with the cops. They gave me a hard time the other day. I just got off probation for some stuff and they acted like I done something to her. I never even saw her."

Tom pulled out the picture and showed it to him.

"Nice-looking chick," the guy replied. "Sorry mister. I don't know anything."

"Did you find anything in the car?" Tom asked.

"No not a thing. Just as I told the cops, it was real clean except for that clay on the tire treads. I noticed it when I was washing the car."

The guy standing next to him lit a cigarette and then blew smoke out and just stood there. Tom noticed Danny started to fidget and Tom looked at the other guy and addressed him.

"You have something you want to say?" Tom asked him.

The other guy looked at Danny and Danny nodded his head at him.

"Well, we found this box full of matchbooks. They were kind of cool. They had these pigs on them, and we didn't want to tell the cops because we figured they would take them. We were laughing because we would be giving the pig matches to the pigs. Get it?"

"Yeah, I get it," said Tom.

The other guy handed him a matchbook. "We don't have any use for cops, and these were in the trunk, so we didn't think the lady left them there. You won't tell the cops will you?" The guy was looking at Tom.

"No" said Tom. "I won't. If it's a clue, I'll use it myself. They haven't been much help anyway."

He looked at the matchbook in his hand. The cover was orange with a pink pig on the cover, dancing around a fire. Bob's Piggy Barn was printed on the cover and below that; THE BEST PORK BARBEQUE IN THE SOUTH.

Tom handed it to his uncle. "You know where this place is?"

"Yep," his uncle answered and then handed the matches back to him.

"Thanks, boys," Tom said.

"Let's go, Uncle Jake. I want to find this place today." They headed off.

"Good luck, mister!" Danny called after him. "I hope you find her soon."

Tom didn't turn around. He felt a chill run up his spine. He hoped he found her soon too.

CHAPTER 9

Sandy was exhausted after yesterday, and when she woke up, it felt like late morning. It was hot inside the place and she had begun to sweat. The little girls were sitting together on the floor and playing with a couple of rag dolls. She hadn't noticed the dolls before. She rubbed her eyes and sat up.

"Are you all right?" she asked them. They both nodded.

"Are you hungry?" Sandy asked.

"No. Mary got us some food while you were sleeping and we went potty."

Sandy turned and looked around for Mary and Lila. She couldn't see them anywhere in the nearby light.

"Where are they?" she asked.

"They went with the lady."

"What lady?" Sandy jumped up and looked around again.

"The lady in the pretty purple robe," Sarah answered. "It was real soft and she let us touch it, but she told us that we had to be very quiet or the father would be mad."

"Stay right here," Sandy said. She began to walk around the entire area looking for another door. The main door made a huge scraping sound when it opened, and Sandy could not believe she would have slept through that. It had woken her up every other time. She had made sure to only eat the fruit and drink tap water in case of the food being drugged. She had done that for the last couple of days, so she was surprised she had dozed off and slept through their leaving. She came back to Rebecca and Sarah.

"Did you see where the woman came from?"

"Up there." Sarah pointed up toward the ceiling. "She told us she was a special angel sent by the father and that if we were good, she would come back and take us with her soon. She said that we would get to play with other children and be in a nice house and have dolls and all kind of toys. She brought us these dolls today."

"She said our mommy had sent her from heaven. Is our mommy in heaven?" They were both looking up at Sandy.

Sandy stared down at their faces and tried to put a smile on her face. "I believe she is in heaven with God. I know she loves you very much and wants you to be safe and go home one day soon and see your daddy."

Both Sarah and Rebecca began to sniffle and Sandy put her arms around them. "Don't cry. We'll be out of here soon. Be brave little girls."

"You'll make a good mother!" Sandy jumped when she heard the booming male voice.

"Who are you?" she shouted. "Where are you?" She turned her head up toward the ceiling.

"I'm here to help you, my child. I hope you're ready to receive your lesson today."

Sandy thought about the previous day and bit her tongue. "Yes," she answered softly. She started to ask about Mary and Lila and then changed her mind. She didn't want to get wet again today. She would wait and ask later.

"Good, we shall begin," the voice answered. "Go get your book of the sacred words."

Sandy walked over and took one of the gold books off the table. She sat down next to Rebecca and Sarah as he began to speak. His voice was droning on in her head as she looked up and tried to focus on his face and then beyond to see where he had come into the building. Surely there was a door up there somewhere.

Maybe tonight she would try to climb up there and look. She knew there had to be a way out. She needed to focus and save her strength. She looked back down at the book as he spoke. He didn't appear to want any responses, so after a while, she just stared at the floor and tried to think about the beach, the sun, anything to not listen to him. She didn't know who he was, but she knew she already hated him, and if given the chance, she would do anything in her power to get them out of there, even if it meant hurting him to do just that. Sandy was surprised she even had those thoughts, but looking over at Rebecca and Sarah and their red-rimmed eyes, she knew she had no choice.

CHAPTER 10

As Tom headed out of the airport for the trip back from Charleston to Myrtle Beach, Jake said, "Tom, it's close to lunchtime. Let's go to downtown Charleston and grab something to eat. I want to show you a place that buys vegetables from our family farm."

"No. I want to get back and find that barbecue place today. I have to find Sandy!" Tom wondered how Jake could even ask such a thing.

"I know, son, how important she is to you," Jake answered. "I promise we'll go there today, but I thought you'd want to see some of the places where your mom and I used to go as children. You know how much your mom loved art and museums. She got that from our visits to Charleston. Our Dad would let us go down to the market in town for a few minutes while he delivered the produce. If you won't stop, how about just riding through. I haven't been down here in years myself."

Thinking about his mom softened Tom's anger at Jake. Tom really wished she were here now. He missed her terribly.

"Okay, but not more than for a few minutes. I can always come back here with Sandy another day." Tom looked at Jake and said, "You can come with us too." He loved his Uncle Jake. Tom had noticed the somber look in Jake's eyes when he talked about his sister. He knew Jake missed her as much as he did. His mom had always said Jake was her hero.

They drove into downtown Charleston and headed toward the river. Jake pointed out the cannons on the South Battery that dated back to the Civil War and Fort Stewart that sat off in the distance across the river. Tom was stunned at the beautiful Southern mansions with the wide wraparound porches and carriage houses out back. Beautiful magnolia trees surrounded them, as did beautiful flowering azaleas and other flowers that Tom did not recognize. When he asked Jake, he said they were oleanders. The houses had ornate wrought iron gates, and the wood trim was carved into intricate patterns that looked like lace. Jake said they were called gingerbread houses. That term seemed to fit, Tom thought. They did look like the gingerbread houses you made at Christmas.

When they got down to the market, Tom was surprised when he had to stop and let a horse-drawn carriage go past. It was like going way back into the past, with carriages on the streets and cobblestone paver roads he had just driven across to reach the market. The buildings were old brick and housed restaurants and lots of shops. Jake said they had once been warehouses that held supplies delivered by the English seafaring ships to the colonies. It truly was a beautiful city. There was so much history here in such an idyllic setting. Tom thought to himself; Sandy and I will have to come here. Thinking of Sandy again made Tom snap out of it. He wanted to get back on the road.

"Let's go, Jake. I want to get back to Myrtle Beach."

Jake nodded and directed him toward the highway to the beach.

They traveled across the huge suspension bridge and Tom marveled at the view of the houses off in the distance. He could see big ships with tons of steel containers going under the bridge. There was an old battleship under the bridge.

All the way back, Jake pointed out landmarks and places he had gone growing up, such as fishing in Georgetown on the river and old abandoned farms that used to belong to his family.

"So many things have changed since I was a young boy," Jake said. "I miss how much fun we used to have at the swimming hole and playing with my cousins. It was so much simpler then."

Tom noticed Jake's shoulders shrunk down, and he seemed really sad.

"You talk like an old man, Uncle Jake," Tom said. "You're only sixty-five years old; that's not exactly ancient, you know."

"Sometimes I feel a hundred," Jake answered. "I sure miss my wife, Cora. She made this world seem not so lost. She was a real sweet one."

That was one of the few times Tom had heard his uncle mention his wife.

Tom knew how awful it would be if he didn't have Sandy in his life. The thought of losing her made him press on the accelerator and speed up some. Who cared if he got a speeding ticket? He just wanted to find her.

When they reached the city limits, Tom looked over at his uncle and asked, "Which way to the barbecue place? You said you knew where it was located."

"Yep, I do. Just keep driving like you're headed out toward my house and I'll tell you where to turn. I don't know if the place is open today or not. I think they only open on the weekends. Good place to eat but not real fancy."

Tom nodded and continued to drive.

"Turn here," his uncle said when they reached a crossroads just a few miles from where the road was to his uncle's house.

They drove for about ten minutes and then Tom spotted the place off to the right. There were a couple of picnic tables sitting out front, but there were no cars and the place looked closed down.

"I can't imagine what she would be doing out here," his uncle said. "Those matches must have been left by somebody else in that car."

As Tom turned in, he noticed a pickup truck partially sticking out from the back of the restaurant. It had something in the back, with sheets pulled over it. He stopped his truck out front and got out.

"Come on, Jake. Let's go see if anybody is here. It looks like someone is out back."

Tom headed around to the back of the place. He reached the truck at the same time someone was coming out of the back of the restaurant carrying a big tray of loaf bread.

The man stopped in his tracks and stared at Tom. Just as Tom started to open his mouth, he heard someone say, "Hold it right there, mister."

Tom turned to see another guy who was holding a shotgun on the other side of the truck. He froze.

Tom put his hands up in the air and stopped where he was standing. "Look, I don't want any trouble. I'm just looking for someone and wanted to ask you a couple of questions."

"Looking for who?" the guy holding the bread asked.

Just then, Tom noticed the guy with the gun look in the direction he had just come from. Jake was walking around the building. The guy dropped the gun down and pointed toward Tom.

"This guy here with you, Jake?"

"Yep, this is my nephew Tom. He's from Colorado. He's Mamie's boy."

"Mamie? Well, I'll be damned!" the guy holding the gun placed it on top of the truck and came around the front.

"You and me are cousins," he said. He held out his hand toward Tom.

Perplexed, Tom looked at him and shook his hand. "What do you mean cousins?"

"Well, my mom and your mom were second cousins. Our mama was Sadie Howard. She talked about Mamie and how much she missed her when she married that northern guy and went away. She wrote us postcards and letters at Christmas, and I know she came to visit once, but she never brought you down here. Mama said Mamie told her that you had allergies, saying that the ragweed and pollen were bad for you, so she left you home. I'm Joe and this is Bubba," Joe pointed toward the guy who had been holding the shotgun.

Tom turned and looked at Jake. Jake was nodding his head and Tom continued to stare at him.

"Why didn't you tell me?" Tom asked.

"Tom, you knew you had kin all over down here. I figured when you moved down this way, we would start the introductions. Many people were upset about your mom leaving and never coming back to visit but once. They felt like she should have married someone from around here and settled down. Most of her family has been around this area their whole lives. But your mom met your dad on a trip to one of those conventions the Walmart sent her to, and well, I guess you know the rest of the story."

Tom did. His mom had told him about standing at the bus stop in the rain after the convention. This man came up next to her and put his umbrella over her head to keep her from getting wet and they had gone for coffee. It was love from there on out. By the end of the week, he had asked her to marry him. He came back two weeks later and off she went to live in Colorado.

His parents had been so in love and he was the only child they ever had. They were both in their thirties when they met. He could remember how they would look at each other and hold hands for hours and just smile. They had such fun, and yes, he had asthma as a child, so they were a little overprotective. Uncle Jake was the only relative he had ever met and his Mom never talked much about home, except how pretty the beaches were, collecting seashells and going on picnics. She had taken him on picnics all the time when he was a child. She carried his medicines and plenty of Benadryl for his allergies. She said she wanted him to love picnics and understand what it was like for her when she was growing up. He had asked her if he had any cousins like the other kids at school. She nodded, but that was it.

His Dad had been an only child also. His grandparents on his Dad's side did take him snow skiing and to Disneyland in California. He had asked his mom about her parents, but she said that they were dead so he would never see them. When he asked if they were in heaven, she always said that she hoped so. When he was older, he asked her what she meant, but she told him that was in the past and said she wouldn't talk about it. Uncle Jake came to her funeral when she died, and Tom had asked him, but he just shook his head and said he would respect his sister's wishes and not talk about them.

Now here he was meeting some long-lost cousins under rather strange circumstances. He wondered if he would get any answers now.

"Come on in, Tom," the one named Joe said to him. "We don't bite."

They all headed into the back of the restaurant. Tom followed them in.

Joe and Bubba both had on overalls and work boots with no shirts. They were freckled, dark-haired, and had brown eyes. Tom thought about how different they looked from his mom. His mother had long blonde hair, deep blue eyes and delicate features. Tom wondered what their mother looked like.

The restaurant had old wood tables, wooden chairs, and chalkboard menus behind the counter. Three different kinds of pork barbecue were listed on the menu, all with different sauces—mustard based, ketchup based, and Bob's secret sauce. There were big plastic containers full of tea, and off to the right was a bar with a couple of stools. There was a cooler filled with beer behind it. He noticed besides the three kinds of barbecue on the menu, the only other items were slaw, rolls, and fixings listed.

"Want a beer?" Joe asked. "We only carry two kinds of beer, Budweiser and Pabst Blue Ribbon. We don't get many calls for fancy stuff here. Mainly local folks and church groups come here on the weekend. We cook up some mean barbecue, though. Slaughter the hogs ourselves."

"Budweiser will be fine," Tom said. He sat down on one of the stools at the counter. "You own this place?"

"No sir. It belongs to our daddy, Percy Howard. We were just loading up some stuff to take on a picnic."

Hearing the word picnic made Tom start thinking about his mom once again and how she loved to go on picnics. "My mom used to tell me about always going on picnics when she was young. She used to take me to the park or lake on a picnic and we always had the best time. She tried to make it extra special. I think she missed being down here and going on picnics or to the beach. We never took a trip to any of the beaches close to where I lived."

They had all turned toward him as he was talking and he noticed that they looked back and forth at each other for a second.

Then Joe said, "Yeah, there's nothing like a family picnic to make you want to whoop and holler and have a good time."

"So what brings you down this way, Tom?" Bubba asked.

"My girlfriend is missing." Tom answered.

"Missing?" Joe asked.

"Yes. She came down here and was staying at a motel and now nobody knows where she is."

"Shame," Bubba was shaking his head side to side. "Is Jake helping you look for her?"

"That's why we're here. Some matches from this place were in the back of the rental car she had. I thought maybe she had been here or somebody here might have seen her or something." Tom pulled her picture and the matches out and showed them to Joe and Bubba.

"We give those out when people come to eat, but like I said, mainly only locals know about this place and come to eat here. We get the occasional tourists and they pick up matches when they leave. Maybe some tourist left them in there."

They both looked at the picture. "Never seen her," they said in unison.

"There was a whole box of matchbooks. It seems like a lot of matches for a tourist to pick up." Tom was looking from Joe to Jake and then at Bubba. They were all looking down at the floor.

"Probably stole them out of the shed. We should keep a better lock on it. It's right out back of here. We put supplies in there until we need them in here." Bubba was pointing out back past the truck and Tom could see an old wooden shed a few yards away.

"Yep, I bet that's it. Couple of college kids stole all of our toilet tissue last summer and put it all over the boathouse down by the creek. That sure was a sight!" Joe and Bubba started laughing.

"Is there anyone else that works here who I could ask about her?" Tom asked.

Both Joe and Bubba looked at the picture again. "She sure is pretty. Sally Ann is the waitress here on the weekend. I guess you could ask her."

"Where is she now?" Tom asked.

"She's at home, but Jake knows right where she lives. He could take you there."

Tom turned toward Jake. "Would you, Jake? I'd like to do it today if possible."

"Okay. Nice seeing you boys. See you in church on Sunday."

"Good luck, Cousin Tom. Come back later this week with Jake and we can get acquainted. Catch up on the last thirty years or so, maybe."

"Sure. I will. I just need to try to find Sandy right now." Tom walked out and realized that Jake had lingered behind. When he turned and looked back, he noticed they were huddled close and talking. Jake looked up just then and waved. Jake hugged both boys then walked out of the restaurant. They headed back to Tom's truck in silence. Tom was still taking in the fact that his mother had never talked about any of these people. She was such a wonderful mom, sweet and loving. He knew she must have had a good reason, but what was it?

CHAPTER 11

Sandy realized she had dozed off for a few minutes after eating what was on the table for supper. It was only bread and fruit. They had listened to the preacher for five hours and her head was still buzzing from the tension in her neck and shoulders. It took all the stamina she had to keep from screaming at him as he droned on. She looked over eat toward the girls.

Lila and Mary were on their beds reading. Sarah and Rebecca were both on one cot, just lying there with their eyes open.

"Gosh, I fell asleep didn't I?" Sandy asked.

They both nodded back at Sandy.

"Do you need to go potty or anything?" she asked the younger girls.

"No. Would you tell us a bedtime story?" Sarah asked.

"Sure. Would you like a story about a pretty princess in a castle?" Sandy asked.

"Yeah," they both said in unison sitting up on the cot.

Sandy walked over and sat down next to them. She instinctively reached out and put her arms around them. They both leaned in against her.

"Once upon a time, there were two beautiful little princesses that were locked away in a castle."

"Like us?" Rebecca asked.

"Yes. Just like you. They had been locked away by a mean old wizard who was mad at the people in their town and he knew everyone would be sad with the little princesses gone. Everyone would miss them and be so sad because they were very special and loved by everyone in the kingdom."

Sarah and Rebecca were staring up at her. They both had hints of smiles on their faces.

Sandy continued talking until both of them began to fall asleep. She gently placed them side by side on the cot. It was hot and Sandy was sweating from the girls just leaning against her, so she put only a towel over them for cover.

She looked around and walked over to Lila and Mary. Lila was the first to look up.

"We shouldn't talk to you. You make the father mad every time he comes. You'll get us in trouble."

"How much more trouble could we be in? We're locked in a shed somewhere, being drugged, hosed down with cold water, and lectured to by some lunatic who thinks he is God Almighty!" Sandy was trying to keep her voice low, but she was seething with anger. "We need to get out of here."

"What the Father says comes from the Bible and isn't bad. The book tells you what the plan is, and if we love the Divine One, then we'll get out of here and live in the world in peace." Lila and Mary were both swaying and nodding as they talked.

Sandy's mouth dropped open. She noticed the look on the girls' faces. Sandy realized that "the Father" had gotten through to them. She wanted to shake them both, but she held back, as she needed them if she was going to work out a plan.

"I'm going to try to find some way to climb up to the top of those rafters tonight and I need you both to help and watch out for the little girls. Will you do that?" she asked.

Lila looked at Mary. Neither one spoke at first. Then Lila said almost in a whisper, "Okay."

"Good. I'm going to wait a couple of hours, until I'm sure it's really late, and then try. I'll wake you up when I do." Sandy turned around and walked back to her cot. She sat down and actually began reading the gold book. It might be useful if she needed to pretend to reference a passage, just in case. *Just in case what?* Sandy wondered. She knew. Just in case she got caught.

CHAPTER 12

Tom and Jake rode in silence all the way toward town and then turned left down a lone dirt road that cut off into the woods form the main road. Jake had driven Tom's truck since he knew the way. He had convinced Tom that it would be easier. After they had gone about five miles down the road, Tom noticed a few trailers on the right, and about one hundred feet past that, Jake turned into the driveway of a little brown trailer. In the front yard there were a couple of deer. They were in the middle of a flower bed full of petunias and pansies. As they got closer, Tom noticed they were statutes. The yard was well groomed and had a little wooden well off to the right. There was a pump next to it. Tom wondered if it was a working pump.

He started to say something, but then the door to the trailer swung open and a blonde woman in short shorts and a t-shirt bounded out. She was waving as the truck came to a stop. Jake waved back and stopped at the end of the driveway. The woman stopped, turned, and looked at Tom. Her arm fell to her side.

"How's it going?" Jake asked as he climbed out of the truck.

The woman walked slowly forward and gave Jake a hug, but her eyes never left Tom's face.

"Sally, this here is my nephew Tom. He is looking for his girlfriend, who went missing, and the boys at the place said he might check with you, seeing as how you waitress on the weekend and she might have been there last week."

"Oh!" She just stood there and continued to stare at Tom.

Tom pulled out a picture of Sandy and held it out toward her. "Do you remember seeing her at all?"

She shook her head no then turned and looked at Jake, who had walked up on the porch. She looked up and down as if sizing him up.

"Got any of your good sweet tea, Sally?"

"Sure, go on in and check the fridge," she answered.

Sally turned and started back toward the trailer. Tom followed without talking. The inside of the trailer wasn't what he expected at all. Sally had on short shorts, yet the inside of her house was filled with religious symbols, crosses and a picture of angels on the wall.

Jake handed Tom a glass filled with tea. He took it.

"Sit down and take a load off," Sally said, pointing toward a brightly flowered couch.

Tom plopped down and sighed as he did.

"You okay?" she asked.

"Just tired, I guess. I was hoping that maybe, just maybe, you had seen my girlfriend. I think she's beautiful and it's hard to believe that no one ever noticed her or remembers her in any of the places she might have been. It's just weird!" He bent down and put his head in his hands.

"Don't worry—we'll keep trying." Jake reached over and patted his shoulder.

Tom looked up, and he could have sworn that just as he did, Sally was winking at Jake, but that didn't make sense. He was tired. Maybe she just had something in her eye, because when she turned toward him, she looked somber.

"Now, you said your girlfriend was in the restaurant?"

"Yes. It would have been last week. She was only here for a few days." Tom pulled out the picture again and showed it to her.

"She does look a little familiar." Sally was nodding her head. "Yeah, seems like I remember her. She ordered some barbecue and tea. Then she asked about Dutton Cove."

"Dutton Cove. What's that?" Tom asked.

"It's a small out-of-the-way saltwater cove in the next town over. It's famous with the locals, as the dolphins love to come in and eat the small minnows that swim there. Lots of people wade out to the sandbar at low tide to watch them. I believe I remember her saying that she wanted to go and see that. I told her how to get there."

"Wow. Uncle Jake, do you think we could go there now?" Tom was starting toward the door.

"Hold on, Tom. You can only go there during the day and it's about dusk now. We couldn't get down the road to that area. It's about thirty miles from here. We can go first thing in the morning. That place is dangerous at dark and high tide."

"Dangerous? What do you mean dangerous?" Tom had a panicked look on his face.

"Well, lots of people have stayed out on that sandbar too long, and when the tide comes in, the current makes it hard to swim back to shore. People have drowned out there!"

"Oh God …" Tom froze in his tracks. His mind was imagining all kinds of bad things that could have happened to Sandy. He shook his head to clear those images away.

CHAPTER 13

Detective Sam Carey was sitting and staring at the pictures on his desk. They were two beautiful little girls. They were all smiles sitting next to each other on the couch dressed up in matching blue dance costumes. Sam turned slowly to look at the wall across the room. There were now a total of ten pictures, all young girls and women that had disappeared in the last year. The pictures on his desk had just been given to him by a distraught woman named Liz Thomas, the victim's sister, and the father, John James, of the missing girls. He had tried to reassure them that they were following every lead, but the glazed blank stare of the man who had just had to identify the body of the woman from the motel as his wife told Sam that they were barely holding on. He had sent both of them with one of his deputies to get some coffee. They both had insisted there was no way that Karen would hang herself. He believed them. They seemed like your average blue collar family. He believed they were sincere, loving and dedicated to each other.

When he had moved here from Georgia to take this promotion, it had taken him time to adjust and accept that things were different in a tourist town.

He had come from a small town in Georgia outside of Statesboro, and while his town had crime, it was never anything like this. There were never multiple missing persons. Most of the time girls and boys that were reported missing were runaways who the police ended up finding at the bus station or maybe over in Statesboro at the college with a group of people they had met at a party.

Their homicide rate was low. The major events that happened in his hometown included domestic disputes, breaking and entering, property damage, drug busts and the occasional gas station robbery.

With Myrtle Beach being a tourist town, he had expected maybe a higher number of runaways or teenagers who didn't return home when they were supposed to after a trip to the beach. Of those he helped investigate in the last five years, the majority of them had always turned up at home eventually.

It seemed to be different now. In the last two years, two adolescent girls and three young women that were reported missing had yet to be found. The FBI, who had assisted in the first few cases, was also stumped. They theorized that someone may be abducting them and disposing of the bodies in the swamp, like the serial killer decades ago who picked up hitchhikers and the bodies were never found. It was always possible they had been taken out of the country for white slavery and prostitution. It was hard for him to accept that in today's world, there were still such things as forced labor and minors being used for illicit purposes.

Every one of the reported missing girls and women had families who loved them and were looking for them. Heck, he still got calls every week from the family of the first young woman who went missing two years ago after a vacation with friends here at the beach. She had walked out onto the main ocean boulevard and was never seen again.

Sam's partner, Chuck Davis, walked back in just then. "Why don't you take a break, Sam? Staring at those pictures only gets you riled up again. Here, have some coffee." He held out the cup.

Detective Carey accepted the coffee. Sam knew the pictures bothered his partner as much as they did him. Chuck had two teenage daughters, twin girls, and since all of this had happened, Chuck had taken off work every time they had a soccer game or any school activity in order to be there. Chuck wouldn't admit it, but Sam had seen the worry on his face, especially when he talked about his daughters' going off to college next year.

Sam had been over to Chuck's house several times to eat. His wife was a schoolteacher. She and Chuck had met in high school in Conway, South Carolina. It was about thirty miles from Myrtle Beach. They had gone to college together and gotten married right out of college. His twin girls were really sweet. They said "Yes, sir" and "No, sir" when Sam went over to visit. Chuck had said they were both straight A students. When Sam asked Chuck if they had boyfriends, he emphatically said, "no, not until they graduate college. That was why he was a police officer and had a gun." They both had laughed at that.

Sam had never married. There had been one girl back home, but she wanted to start a family right away and he didn't. After that, he got promoted and moved away. He was married to his job now.

"Thanks for the coffee, Chuck. My eyes were starting to blur. I was reviewing everything we have on the

Karen James case so far. The fact that she would just up and come here with her two little girls and not tell her family, well, it does not seem to fit her profile at all. Every friend and relative we interviewed said she was a good Christian woman and really loved her girls. She would not leave them alone in this world. Plus, part of her belief was that suicide was a sin."

"I don't know, Sam. I can remember back when I was a kid we used to leave our doors unlocked. Everyone would stop to help you if you had a flat tire or bring a truck to help you move stuff. You knew everybody on the street. We all trusted each other. Now everyone looks at any stranger with suspicion. It has become a mysterious, violent world out there. I know some of this kind of stuff was probably going on then, but you just didn't hear about it. We felt safe and secure at night. Now I recheck the doors and windows at least twice before I go to bed. I'm more nervous about it than my wife. Ain't that a kick in the head?"

"Yes, it is, Chuck. Especially considering that you outweigh your wife by one hundred pounds and you're the scaredy-cat!"

Chuck laughed loudly.

Sam had the feeling that there wouldn't be any good news or anything to laugh about for a while. He shook his head and again stared at the pictures. What the hell had happened to these girls and women? It was as if a spaceship had landed and taken them off the planet.

CHAPTER 14

Tom tossed and turned all night and woke at six in the morning. He crawled out of bed, made some coffee in his room and then decided he would head out on his own. Uncle Jake had said he would pick him up at nine, but Tom felt a need to go out on his own.

There were way too many good old boys around here and he had the feeling he wasn't getting straight answers. His dad had told him that down South they had what was called "the good old boy" syndrome. Everybody stuck together and everyone was distantly related. They supported each other in politics and the police department. They were all of a like mind.

After Tom got dressed, he got in the truck and headed back down the highway until he reached the place where Jake had pointed out to turn to reach Dutton Cove. He drove about fifteen miles and then the road divided. He decided to go right. He saw a handmade wooden sign after he turned: DUTTON COVE TEN MILES. It would be easy to miss unless you knew where you were going. When he got to the end of the road, there were already a couple of cars parked in the dirt parking area off to the left and he saw a path that led through some brush ahead. There was another wooden sign: TO DUTTON COVE.

He parked, got out, and headed down the path. It was a beautiful path with palms and ferns lining the way; although well worn, it still gave the feeling that you were alone in a tropical jungle.

The path widened at the end and then opened out onto a small beach area about a half mile wide, with white sand and there were small waves gently lapping up onto the sandy beach.

There was actually a small building off to the right of the sand. It looked as if it had been constructed by locals, with a fire pit and a couple of trash barrels. Painted on the trash barrels were the words PLEASE PICK UP YOUR TRASH.

He saw five people around fifty yards out, standing on what looked like a sandbar. They were laughing, then looked up and waved at him. They had placed their beach chairs, coolers, and towels on the sand. Tom figured they must have waded out. It couldn't be that deep.

He had worn shorts, so he pulled off his shoes and started to wade out. The ground sloped down and he actually got up to waist deep. So much for keeping dry he thought. He could feel the suction of the sand under his feet. When he got to the sandbar, the group was looking at him as if he were nuts for wading out in his clothes.

"Deeper than you thought, huh?" one of the guys asked.

"Yeah, sure was," he answered. He looked down at his wet clothes.

"You come to see the dolphins?" the same guy asked.

"No. I was just looking the place over. Someone told me about it. You guys come out here much?" Tom asked the two men standing next to him.

"Usually every weekend," one of them answered. "We like the quiet and most of the dolphins will swim right up to us at low tide. We always bring some fish in our coolers."

Tom looked down and noticed that they each had a baggie of raw fish in their hands. Tom looked at the water but didn't see any dolphins.

"No dolphins today?" he asked.

"No. Sometimes if the river plant about five miles down is doing a lot of activity out on the water, they don't show up. We figured that out after talking to one of the game and fish wardens one day. He said they don't like the noise or maybe they don't like what is going on at the plant. Dolphins are pretty smart, you know. A lot of people have picketed that plant for not being environmentally friendly. They have never proven that they're dumping in the water, but some people say they do release chemicals at night. Don't know. We just know that the dolphins don't come some weekends and the minnow don't seem to come into the beach area. Today is one of those days."

"I hear it can get rough out here at high tide. Is that true?" Tom asked.

"Yeah, man. We got caught out here once at high tide when a storm was coming in and Randy here got pulled under. It gets several feet deeper and the water seems to swirl from left to right. We've been careful since then and only come at low tide. We were lucky one of the girls had brought a float that day and we were able to make a chain of people and get Randy out."

"Ever hear of anyone drowning recently here?" Tom asked.

"Not since that little girl five years ago. She was out here with her parents and they fell asleep on the beach. She came back out to the sandbar. By the time she was yelling it was too late. They tried but couldn't get to her in time. It was like a swirling riptide. It was really sad. They closed the place off for a while, but mainly only locals come out here anyway. The game and fish people ride by on weekends and check it out. I've never seen more than twenty-five people out here at any one time. It's on state land, but a lot of the locals come and do cookouts and stuff with their families. It's too dark to stay out here at night and there are a lot of creepy-crawly critters around."

"Thanks," Tom said. He started wading back in. He really couldn't picture Sandy coming out here by herself, plus he wondered who she would have heard about it from. If only mostly locals came here, then she would probably stick to the public beaches. Maybe Sally was wrong and it was another woman who asked her about Dutton Cove. Regardless, he felt that it was another dead end. He needed to get back to Myrtle Beach and start looking other places for Sandy.

CHAPTER 15

After Tom left Dutton Cove, he just began to drive with no definite destination in mind. He should call Uncle Jake. He looked down and realized he had left his cell phone at the motel. Then he wondered about the rest of his mother's family. He knew she had lots of relatives besides the ones he had met the other day at the restaurant. Why not look some of them up and see if they could help out?

He started thinking back to some of the things he had heard his mother say about where she grew up, like the big picnics they would have and the church socials where the whole family was together. He remembered his father saying one time that his mother had enough relatives to make up a small town. Surely there were some he could find.

He stopped at the first gas station he came to and looked for a pay phone. He had noticed that down here there were a lot more pay phones or public phones than there were up North. He found the name Simmons—it covered more than two pages—and he saw Jake's name and number when he was going through it. He saw a

Lottie Simmons and for some reason that name rang a bell, so he dialed the number. A woman answered and Tom said, "Hi, my name's Tom Barton. Did you have a sister named Mamie Summer Simmons?" He heard the woman suck in her breath, and then she said, "Who is this?"

"Are you her sister?" he asked.

"Yes. I'm her older sister, Lottie May Simmons. Now, who are you?"

Tom didn't know why, but he blurted out, "May I come and see you? I'm her son, your nephew."

"Oh lord, yes! I sure have missed seeing your Mom over the years. All your kin will be excited to know you are here. You come right on over. Let me give you the directions."

Tom got back in his truck and started driving. Tom thought to himself that it was odd his Uncle Jake had not mentioned going to see his family to get them to help out finding Sandy. Tom didn't know what he was going to say when he got there, but he had a burning curiosity now to find out something about his mother's family and also to feel like as if belonged somewhere.

Jan Sylve

It took him forty-five minutes to get to the house out in the country. There was a long winding road with fences on each side and he could see cattle and barns off in the distance. It looked so peaceful and serene. He wondered why his mother didn't want to come back here to visit more often. She had just said they were upset when she left and could not forgive her for marrying a Yankee. Then she and his father would laugh.

When he drove up, a woman walked out onto the porch. He couldn't see her face well, but her shape and long hair reminded him of his mother. She stopped on the top stair. He walked up to her and stuck out his hand. "I'm Tom."

She took his hand and held it tightly for a minute, looking in his eyes. "You got your mama's eyes. They are so pretty and blue. That's why she was named Summer, you know. I guess she used her first name, Mamie, when she moved away." She dropped his hand. "Come on in. Lots of people want to meet you."

When Tom went in, he could not believe that there were about twenty people standing in the front room. In addition to Joe and Bubba, whom he had met the other day, there were some teenagers along with lots of men and women. They took turns approaching Tom

116

and making introductions. It turned out that two of the men were his mother's brothers and three of the other women her sisters. Many of the other adults were his first cousins. He was overwhelmed. They all seemed genuinely glad to see him.

Tom plopped down on the sofa. "I never knew Mother had such a large family. I'm in shock," he said.

They all nodded.

"You want to see some pictures of your mom growing up?" Lottie asked.

"Yes, I would like that." He looked around the room. Lots of old pictures and he noticed that there were religious figures and crosses on the small tables.

Lottie picked up a photo album she had on the table and started flipping the pages. His mother was a beautiful baby. She was smiling and sitting with her sisters in the couch and on a blanket outside somewhere. He noticed that as she got older, she smiled less and looked more serious, but she was always in the company of her sisters, brothers and often sitting in the room he was in now. There were a lot of pictures in the fields or in a barn. She had long flowing blonde hair and those beautiful blue eyes. In the last few pictures, she was in a fancy white dress and holding a Bible.

Lottie noticed his look and said, "Our dad was a preacher and our mom was a Sunday school teacher. We dressed up to go to church every Sunday."

Tom sat there with his mouth open. His mother had never mentioned anything about her parents being in the church, especially her dad being a preacher.

"I had no idea. Mom never said a word about that. She just said her parents were dead." Tom looked from Lottie to the others as they exchanged glances.

"Well, Tom, your mom sort of had a falling out with Dad and she left when she was thirty. When Mom and Dad died, she didn't come back for the funeral."

Tom could hardly believe his ears. His mom was so sweet and loving. He just couldn't imagine that she would not want to come home when her parents died. His thoughts were interrupted by Lottie speaking.

"She loved them, Tom. Don't get me wrong; we know she loved them. It's just that some wounds don't heal that easily. I guess she was probably pregnant with you at the time. You're in your twenties, I would guess, right?"

"Yes. My birthday's this month. I'll be twenty-eight."

"It's all in the past now. Anyway, we are sure glad to see you. I missed her so much. We were the closest and I lost my best friend when she left." Tears were welling up in Lottie's eyes. Tom put his arm around her and she leaned in on his shoulder.

They all chatted away and asked a million questions about what he did and what it was like growing up for him. They wanted to know about where he lived and what his dad and mom did in Colorado. Three hours had passed before Tom knew it. He had shown them the couple of pictures of his mom and dad that he carried in his wallet and they had all passed them around. Someone made sweet tea, sandwiches and brought them out on a platter for everyone. He was feeling right at home.

When he left about sundown, he couldn't help wondering why his mother never talked about her family. It made no sense. He wished his mom and dad were still alive. He especially missed his mom. They were very close. Maybe he would ask Uncle Jake why his mom never really wanted to come home. There had to be something more to it than just a falling out with her parents.

When Tom got back to the motel, he decided to go to the office and let them know he would be staying at least another week. After that, well, he just didn't know. He felt lost and more confused than ever.

CHAPTER 16

Sandy had pretended to be asleep until all the girls were out like a light. She could see moonlight filtering in from the skylights in the roof above. She went over to the wall farthest away from the sleeping girls.

She had made a homemade length of rope out of a bedsheet. She knew it would not be very strong, but she might find a way to use it. It was only about six feet long wound together in strips. Sandy had broken off the heads on two of the thickest plastic spoons that had come with their meals. She hoped the ends would stick into the wooden beams she had found on this side of the room to give her leverage and footholds to get up the wall. The rest of the walls were metal, so she didn't have much hope of climbing up those.

She felt the post. It wasn't hard, but not yet rotted. She took out one of the spoon handles and pushed with all her might. It went into the wood about half an inch. She backed up and pushed again with the bottom of her foot. It went in about another half an inch.

She put her hands on both sides of the beam and started to climb. She was able to get a bit of a foothold with the handle and then it started to bend. She gripped her bare feet as best she could on both sides. She would try to shinny up some more.

It was painstakingly slow and she only could go up an inch at the time. Splinters were getting into her hands and feet, but Sandy refused to give up. She pulled out the other handle and stabbed it into the wood. It gave her a handhold with one hand and didn't bend back before she pulled it out and stabbed again. She heard one of the girls whimper in her sleep and she froze. Then she heard nothing but silence again.

She was sweating profusely and was only about halfway up. Her back and legs ached, and her hands were bleeding now from the times she started to slip. Just when she thought she could not hold on, she saw what looked like a metal hook about three feet above her head, sticking out of the wall. She had the sheet rope around her neck and she thought if maybe she could let one hand go and swing it up over the hook, she could pull up that way. She gingerly let go with one hand, but she started to slide.

She got a better grip with her feet and then tried again. She swung it several times, and finally it caught over the top of the hook. She pulled down on it with the one hand and it felt secure. She used the sheet rope and her feet to make it up the rest of the way, until she was even with the hook.

She was exhausted by now and she just hung there for a while to rest. She actually started to nod off—probably all the adrenalin was wearing off—so she started up again. She reached the top peak where the roof started to pitch and there was a beam that ran across the length of the room. She was finally able to stand. She felt dizzy but steadied herself and headed out onto the beam.

She reached the point under the skylight and could barely stand on her tiptoes and touch it. It didn't feel like heavy glass. She was standing there trying to decide how she was going to break it and get out when she heard a scream. She looked down into the dark and saw Lila standing beneath her.

"No, Sandy, don't go!"

She shushed Lila and then heard one of the other girls cry out, "Don't leave us! You promised."

She whispered, "I'll come back for you."

At that moment, she heard a swooshing sound and turned to see a tackle block and hook come swinging at her. She lost her balance, reached out, and felt nothing but air. As she began to fall, she heard Lila and Mary screaming. Then there was only blackness.

CHAPTER 17

Sandy woke up and tried to sit up. She was just able to raise her head. She looked down and noticed that she was tied to a cot and when she looked around, she could tell she was in some kind of metal shed, like a toolshed. The floor was cement and the wall looked like rusted old metal. There was a battery-operated lamp in the corner on a table. She heard a door open behind her and she craned her neck to see a woman in a white dress walking toward her carrying a tray. Sandy had a pounding headache and she lay back down as the room began to spin a little bit.

"Well, I see you're awake now. I bet your head is hurting plenty." The woman stood over her and shook her head. "Let's see if we can clean you up a little bit. You've got a nasty bump and bruise on your head and scrapes on your legs and back."

The woman pulled up an old metal chair and sat down next to her. She put a cloth in some water and started to wipe Sandy's head. The water was warm and felt good, so Sandy didn't pull away. It felt nice to have someone being kind to her and she didn't want to let that feeling go just this minute. Finally the woman washed her whole face and then drew back to look down at Sandy.

"You're a pretty girl and lucky this probably won't leave a scar. You may not be so lucky next time and I don't know why you would want to run away. The father is offering you a better life here and a chance to do God's work. There is no greater gift on earth than doing the work of the Divine One."

The woman seemed to stare off into space and then her gaze came back down to Sandy. "You'll have to stay here until you're ready to accept that." She stood up and walked to the table.

"Wait. May I get some food or go to the bathroom?" Sandy pleaded. She could feel her stomach beginning to growl. She was hungry and had no idea what time it was or if it was night or day.

The woman didn't turn around. She placed the tray on the table and then turned toward the door.

"Please wait," Sandy said.

The woman kept going and shut the door behind her.

CHAPTER 18

Tom was tired. He had slept fitfully all night, with strange dreams along with images of his mom sitting in a dark room. He got up at five in the morning and decided to take a walk. He passed the office and saw that no one was at the front desk. He opened the door and went in. He called out, "Anybody here?"

No one answered. He noticed a light coming from the back room, so he walked in there and called out again. No one answered. It was dark, but he noticed a light coming from what appeared to be a hole in the back wall. He walked over to take a look, and when he touched the hole, a panel in the wall opened and he was facing a small corridor that looked as if it led to another room. He started to step back and then figured what the heck; he headed down the small hall. At the end was a room that was dark. He felt around and found a light switch on the wall and turned it on.

In the middle of the room was an old-time pulpit and all around the room were posters, some peeling off the walls, some not, with pictures of religious symbols, crosses, and groups of people kneeling below a man in dark clothes. There were several shelves of books and Bibles and all kinds of offering plates stacked on the floor. He remembered that they used to pass one around at the church when he was a child. His mom had told him that tithing to the church was important. Then one day she suddenly stopped going and would never go back. She would not answer him when he asked why and his dad just got quiet and looked out the window.

He walked over to look at one of the posters. A group of people in white gowns were kneeling at the cross, and a man standing at the bottom of the cross had his hands raised high as he faced the people. The more he stared, the more he thought the man looked familiar. Then he realized it looked an awful lot like his Uncle Jake, but that couldn't be. He was leaning over looking closely when he heard someone come in behind him. He turned to see a shadow and then there was this horrible smell. It was really strong and he felt dizzy. As Tom fought back against someone grabbing him, something hit him on the head. He fought back a minute more and then things went black.

CHAPTER 19

Tom came to and found himself lying in a big four-poster bed. He could see the sunlight filtering in through the curtains and there was a smell of fresh-cut grass on the breeze.

He rolled over on his back. His head hurt and his mouth was dry. He licked his lips and then tried to get to his feet. He was woozy. Just then, he heard voices, and the door opened. In the doorway were his Uncle Jake and Lottie.

"You're awake. How are you feeling?" Lottie asked. "Like crap! What the hell is going on?" Tom replied.

"Just hold on," Jake said. He walked toward the bed.

"Simmer down, son, and we can explain," Lottie said.

"The manager at the motel thought you were a prowler. He is actually one of your distant kin. He runs the motel for his aunt. Her husband died a few years ago. He was going to call the police and then his aunt came in and told him who you were. I had called her yesterday to let her know you were Summer's son. He feels really bad about it. He hit you over the head."

"What was that awful stuff I smelled?" Tom asked.

"Oh, Lucas had been cleaning up out back and had some cleaning solution on his hands. He hit you with the broom he had been cleaning with. You must have smelled the cleaning solutions. He feels really, really bad. He owes you a personal apology. His aunt called me and we went and picked you up in Jake's truck. We decided you needed to come out here in the country with us and stay a while. You'll be better off staying with your kinfolk out here and we can help you look for your woman."

"It seems like you kidnapped me!" Tom said angrily. "I need to get out of here and go look for Sandy." Tom tried to stand up again.

"Settle down, Tom. We're going to help you, but you have to promise not to go running off like some wild animal we have to snare," Lottie said with a smile. Jake just stood there.

Tom looked at Jake's serious face and for a minute, the thought crossed his mind that they might just do that, hunt him like a wild animal.

Tom made it to his feet this time and staggered toward the door. Jake stood back and let him out. He made it as far as the couch in the living room and then he plopped down. His cousins Joe and Bubba were sitting across from him. They smiled and nodded.

CHAPTER 20

Detective Carey had been working on Karen and Sandy's cases with an FBI agent named Harry Carlton. They had interviewed at least fifty people in the last week. They started with all the desk clerks at the motel, then the housekeeping staff, landscapers and maintenance crew. The FBI agent had interviewed the old woman who owned the motel. Her name was Gertie Brown. Her room was musty, he had told Detective Carey, and she had two cats that walked all over her furniture. He told Sam that she said that after her husband died, her nephew came to run the place. He would inherit it when she died.

She and her husband had bought the motel twenty years ago from a family from India who sold out to go back up North. They had fixed up the rooms, restaurant and bar when they first bought the place. Mrs. Brown told him that they barely had enough money to keep up the maintenance of the pool and tourist areas. Agent Carlton told Sam that it didn't look as if her small one-bedroom apartment behind the desk had been touched in twenty years. The rooms above the office were for storage and one small room where the nephew lived. It had a kitchenette. It was pretty shabby and only had a shower stall and toilet. The other two rooms up there had old beds, supplies and mattresses. The police had gone over all the rooms and the whole motel looking for clues or anything unusual, but they didn't find anything significant.

Any person who had worked at the Eastside Inn in the last six months was contacted and interviewed in person or by phone. A couple of the maintenance crew had prior arrests, but they had solid alibis for the weekend Karen had died and her daughters had gone missing. One maid had reported seeing an older man in a gray van circling the parking lot two days before they went missing. A similar van had also been reported in the past, when two teenage girls had gone missing on the ocean boulevard last year. They had followed up all leads and surveillance video, with no luck.

The Eastside Inn didn't have any security cameras except at the front entrance. Detective Carey and Agent Carlton had looked at those, but the video was grainy. It was a very old VHS system.

Detective Carey had finally tracked down the sponsor of the dance competition in Charleston the weekend in question and he was headed down there to conduct interviews with some of the staff. He had also asked for names of the other contestants in the girls' age group as well as those of their parents. Maybe Karen James had said something to one of them. He had asked those parents that were local to the area if they could come to the art center to meet. Two weeks had gone by now and he realized that people tended to forget more as time passed.

Detective Carey arrived at the art center in Charleston early in the morning.

He met with the chairman of the Southeastern Lights Dance Competition Event. His name was John Stanson. He told Detective Carey up front that their organization didn't allow solicitation at their events. Sponsors could set up booths in the lobby, but they were checked out to make sure they were legitimate and reputable. Often it might be modeling agencies or other advertising agencies that might want to recruit young girls for movies or entertainment events, like local tourist productions or plays.

"What about people who buy tickets to the event?" Detective Carey asked.

"Well, we can't control every person that comes through the door. We have to rely on the parents to make smart decisions for their children and we provide information on the sponsors we do have," Mr. Stanson told him.

Detective Carey showed him the pictures of the victim and her daughters and asked if he remembered them. He did not.

While he was interviewing the support staff, one of the women said she remembered Ms. James. "I remember her because she had such pretty red hair and I have red hair, so I went up and spoke to her," she told him.

"Did you see her talking to anyone in particular?" Sam asked.

"Well, there was this one man. I remember because he was dressed all in black. He had on a black suit, black tie, black shoes. It's pretty hot this time of year in Charleston, so you don't see many people dressed all in black."

"Do you remember anything else about him?" Sam asked.

"Now that you mention it, I walked by him and overheard him telling Ms. James something about a movie. I never saw him again after that. I thought it might have been someone she knew. Sorry, I wish I could be of more help."

"Thanks," Sam said. "If you think of anything else, please give me a call." Sam handed both of them one of his cards.

Detective Carey only had a couple of more participants and parents to interview. A woman walked up to him just as he was finishing talking to the staff assistant.

"Did I hear you say something about a man in black?" she asked.

Detective Carey turned and looked at her. "Yes. Did you know that man?"

"No. However, a man dressed like that came up to me at the competition and said he was making a commercial about children on a farm for a children's network channel and wondered if my daughter might like to be in it. He had seen my daughter dancing in the competition. I asked him where it was being filmed and if he had a card to give me. I remember he said they would be filming somewhere outside of Myrtle Beach. He said he worked with movie productions companies in Myrtle Beach and Wilmington, North Carolina. He gave me a card with his name and number on it, but when I called, the number went to voicemail and I left a message. I never heard anything back. I might still have the card in my pocketbook." She started to rummage around in her purse.

Detective Carey could not believe his luck. This was the first solid lead they had gotten on any suspect.

"Here it is." The woman handed him a white business card. Printed on it was the name Jonathan Stokes. The card listed his business as Candlelight Productions. There was an address in Savannah, Georgia, a phone number, and a website.

"Is it possible you would recognize this man if you saw him again?" Sam asked the woman.

"I think so. I only talked to him for a couple of minutes. After he handed me the card, I told him I could not come up to Myrtle Beach to meet him. He left after that. As I said, I called the number and it went to voicemail. Something didn't feel right about it. I had forgotten all about it until I heard you talking to Ms. Powell just now."

Detective Carey went back to Mr. Stanson and asked him if they had security cameras in the convention center. He said most of them were pointed toward the parking lot, but a few were in the lobby area. He called the chief of security and directed Detective Carey to that area. Sam watched the tapes with the security chief and on one camera from the lobby area, he noticed a redheaded woman talking to a tall, slim man dressed in black. The figure reminded Detective Carey of the "slim man" character he had seen on TV in another case out in the Midwest. The thin man lured young girls to him so they would do his bidding. That gave him the creeps. The man in black was turned to the side, so all Sam could make out was gray hair and long sideburns. In the video standing next to the man was a woman dressed in a white pantsuit. She had her hair pulled back in a bun, but that was all Sam could tell for sure.

Sam asked for a copy of the recording to take back to Myrtle Beach with him. Maybe the FBI could work with it and get a better quality picture of the suspect and the woman's face. Sam put the card in a baggie in his pocket. He would give it to Agent Carlton to run for fingerprints.

CHAPTER 21

The business card that Sam had gotten from the woman in Charleston had been analyzed and all prints compared with the FBI database. They didn't get any matches. The video, even when cleared up, didn't give a good look at the man's face. They ran it through the facial recognition software and it didn't match any mug shots on file. They did get a hit on the female standing next to him. She had been arrested in Atlanta and Savannah, Georgia, for prostitution. Her name was Betty Usher.

Agent Carlton drove to Savannah with the pictures of both the man and the woman downloaded from the videotape. He located the address on the card and there was a tattoo parlor on the bottom of the building and rental rooms above it. The agent questioned people in the neighborhood and one man at the corner grocery knew the woman. "That's crazy Betty," he said. "She used to live in one of those rooms above the tattoo parlor. She swept the streets for us sometimes to get enough money to buy wine and then she would turn tricks for money. She got busted several times and ended up in a halfway house."

The grocer went on to say, "I didn't see her for several years and then one day she just showed up dressed real nice and said she had been saved and had a good job. I was shocked."

"Did she say what job she had?" Agent Carlton asked.

"Yes," the grocery owner said. "She said she was working for an ad agency here in town, helping find people to star in movies. I thought she was making it up, but she showed me a business card for some company and then she left. That was about two months ago."

"Thanks. If you see her or hear anything else about her, give me a call." The agent handed him a card. He went back to the tattoo parlor to ask the landlord if he could see the room where she stayed. The owner refused. "I know my rights, you got to have a warrant," he glared at Agent Carlton and crossed his arms.

"Well, I can easily get one buddy, but if you cooperate, it will make both our lives a lot easier." Carlton glared right back.

"The guy shifted back and forth in his chair, looked around a minute, then said. "Listen, mister, that room has someone in it right now. If you would come back tomorrow, say around ten a.m., I could make sure no one was there. Okay?"

Carlton nodded. He wondered to himself if this guy had anything to hide, but noticing some of the people going in up the stairs, it might just be the room was being used for hourly purposes based on the women he saw.

"Okay. I'll be back tomorrow at ten a.m. prompt. Don't make me wait around. Is that clear?" Carlton had leaned in very close to the man.

"Yeah, it's clear," the landlord appeared to relax his posture and his demeanor changed.

Carlton spent the rest of the day checking out homeless shelters and local ad agencies along with movie production companies. There were quite a few in Savannah. A lot of movies had been filmed in this town. Savannah was beautiful, with lots of historic homes, cobblestone streets, Spanish moss hanging from the trees and public parks throughout the town. This was one assignment he didn't mind. He remembered that the movies *Midnight in the Garden of Good and Evil* and *Forrest Gump* had been filmed here. Agent Carlton decided that on his next vacation, he would bring his family here from Virginia. No one at any of the production companies or ad agencies had ever seen Betty or the man in black.

He ate out on the river downtown that night, had a couple of drinks then crashed out by ten p.m.

He went back the next day and the landlord at the tattoo parlor handed him the key right away. The room was a real dump. It had a bed that looked like it came on a covered wagon, a small dirty kitchen and separate bathroom with rusted pipes, a torn shower curtain and indescribable stains in the sink. He searched all the drawers, under the unmade bed and felt for loose floorboards. He went back downstairs. The landlord was much more pleasant today. He said Betty had just left one day with a man and never come back. He looked at the picture Carlton showed him of the man in black, but the landlord said he could not tell if that was him. He did remember the man had gray hair and said he was from up North. That was two year ago. The only thing Betty had left behind was a gold book that was worn out and worthless. He had given it to the used bookstore down the street. The landlord gave him the name of the bookstore and Carlton thought he would go check it out.

CHAPTER 22

Sandy had lost track of time. She realized it had probably been about four weeks since she had tried to run away. Three days ago, she had been brought back to the original building where she was when she had first been brought here. The older girls, Lila and Mary, now were dressed up every evening for some ceremony and escorted to the main house after supper. Often a woman would come now instead of the father to give the lessons from one to three in the afternoon. Sandy sat with Sarah and Rebecca and they just listened every day. Sandy sat on her cot and never made a sound. She didn't want to go back into that dark shed in isolation again. They had only brought her food and water once each day and she had to use the bathroom on the floor.

About a week later, Lila did not come back with her sister that night. Mary said she was with the father now.

Sandy decided she would continue to bide her time, reading the book every night and pretending to listen when the father or the other woman came to give the lesson. The father still stood up in the rafters when he came. Sandy had decided by now that Tom must not be able to find her. She held onto the belief that he was still looking. That was the only thing that kept her going. Sandy also never let go of the hope of escaping. She would find a way to get Rebecca and Sarah out of here with her when she went, if it was the last thing she ever did.

CHAPTER 23

During the several weeks that had passed, Tom spent all his time with his cousins out on the farm, doing chores in the morning and going to town and looking for anyone who might have seen or noticed Sandy. He checked in with Detective Carey and always got the same answer: no new leads. Tom had taken a leave of absence from work. He had called the company in Pawley's Island and told them he could not take the job at this time. They told him to let them know if he was still interested in the future.

Tom felt at home with his relatives. They were like the brothers and sisters he never had. Lottie was like a second mom to him and he enjoyed their big meals at night, which they referred to as family supper. He had to go out and buy jeans and new clothes. He had gained ten pounds, but it was mostly all muscle from working outside.

Tom had gone with his family many times now to their little rural church right down the road. The preacher had a way about him. He had a gentle, kind look about him, which reminded him of a grandfatherly figure. He was mesmerizing when he spoke about all the evil in the world. His message was that people should return to the simple life, work the land and serve God. Blessings would always follow if you lived that way. The real true blessings, he said, were your family and your children. Always give to the Divine One what was his and do not crave the materialistic things in life. Those things always led people to do what was wrong in God's eyes. Tom really liked him and he came over to the house some nights to share family supper. Something about him made you feel like you had known him all your life. Jake only came over every once in a while. He said he was busy with his own little garden. Tom didn't mind. They sat around and sang songs at night and played bible trivia games. They didn't even have a TV, just a radio.

CHAPTER 24

Sandy was alone in the cleansing shed now. A week ago, Rebecca and Sarah had been moved to the main house to start classes with children their own age. Before they had gone, Sandy noticed they seemed calmer and happier. They rarely asked about their mother anymore. That worried Sandy.

The elder women now allowed Sandy to come to the main house for a couple of hours a day with an armed escort. On her way there, she had noticed that there were several buildings around the main house. The building they first took her to had a kitchen and a huge pantry. Her job was to help cook occasionally and then clean the main house. The main house had classrooms and she had seen children and adults in each of those rooms. In the kitchen, they had three wood stoves, but in the main house there was modern electricity and plumbing. Sandy had noticed right off that there were no telephones anywhere that she could see. No cars were ever parked in the yard either.

Bookshelves with reading materials, puzzles, and fabric with sewing supplies had been placed in the shed where she slept. She had gone to help cook one day and come back and all of it was there. She had made herself a couple more cotton dresses from the material they brought. The women took the scissors back out every night when they brought supper and gave them back in the morning with breakfast.

Sandy had struck up a conversation with one of the women who brought supplies. Her name was Lydia. She was nice and spoke very softly. She had even gotten some soap and skin lotion when Sandy asked for it. She told Sandy that she was one of the father's daughters. When Sandy asked if she had any brothers or sisters, she had answered that they were all her brothers and sisters.

Lydia walked with a limp and it often took her a while to get from the door to the living areas of the building. Over the last few days, Sandy had started to time how long it took her to cover the distance. She knew she could outrun her back to the open door, and the last couple of times, she saw another woman waiting outside the door instead of a man.

Lydia must have read her mind to a degree, for she said, "I don't walk as fast as I used to. I miss taking long walks down by the pond."

"What happened?" Sandy asked.

"I fell off a roof."

"God, that had to hurt," Sandy said.

"Yes, but I learned my lesson." Lydia answered.

"What do you mean?" Sandy asked.

"Nothing," Lydia hung her head. "I just know that I'm not blessed like the others are."

The other woman who stood at the door came in. "Hush, Lydia," she said. The woman looked at Sandy. "Would you like to start working outside in the fields?" she asked.

"Yes," Sandy answered enthusiastically. She wasn't too keen on helping in the kitchen. Being outdoors was what she loved.

"Good. I'll ask the father. I think you're ready."

"Thank you," Sandy said. She realized that she truly was thankful. She would do anything to get out of the shed more than a couple of hours a day.

CHAPTER 25

Sandy had finally been moved into the main house. She was in a room with Sarah. She had to get up every morning at six to go work in the fields. They were only allowed to come back in at eight for breakfast after they completed their work in the field. Sandy looked up at the sun as she continued to pick peas. She loved being outdoors. She went through her days and only thought about the outside world once in a while. For the moment, she had given up trying to escape. When they had let her come out to the fields, she had seen all the guards, fences, and noticed they were way out in the middle of the woods. One of the elder women who had been there fifty years told her that no one had ever run away. They would be punished. Plus, she had Sarah to look out for and she couldn't leave her. Rebecca had been taken to another house two weeks ago, so Sarah had clung to her a little more ever since.

Sandy had noticed that way down at the end of the field was a huge barn with trucks and cars coming and going out of it. One of the other young women in the field with her told her they sold some of the produce in the community to raise money for the father's work. They were surrounded by fields and woods off in the distance, so Sandy could see how they could make some money. There was much more than was needed to feed all the people here and the pantry was loaded with vegetable and fruits that had been canned. Sandy estimated that between all the buildings, there were about seventy-five people here on this farm. Some of the buildings were farther away from the main house and the elders lived in those. She was told that the father had his own place farther back in the woods. Sandy had never seen him up close. He spoke on Sundays at the pulpit, but the pulpit was again way up in rafters at the small church on the property and you could only hear his voice and occasionally see a flash of a purple robe. Lydia had told her that was so he could be close to the Divine One when he spoke to the father and sent him visions.

Then the father passed the word down to his disciples and followers.

One week ago, one of the elders, Mable, had come to the kitchen and said Lydia had gone on to Heaven. The men had buried Lydia in the field two days later and wildflowers were already beginning to grow on the mound. One of the male elders said that was a sign of the end of Lydia's wild life; she was with the Divine One now. Sandy wondered what happened to her but never asked. One of the women had just said it was her time to pass on.

Sandy daydreamed a lot, even in the gathering hour. She tried to listen to the father on Sundays when he spoke, but her mind always wandered. All she could think about was being outdoors. She had some squirrels she fed when she was in the adult classes at night. The squirrels came up to the open window and she snuck crackers out to them. Sometimes they would sit there for ten minutes as though listening as the elders droned on and one about the great reward awaiting all of them with the Divine One. The majority of the time in class, the elder women just read aloud from the gold book.

Occasionally Sandy could see a deer off in the distance out of the window in her bedroom.

She never wore shoes anymore and laughed when she thought about all those high heels she had left back home. *Home* that word seemed strange. This was her home now. Then she would think of Tom and shake her head. No more, no more. She couldn't think like that or she would be like the bad ones and be punished. She started to hum one of the good songs and soon her mind was empty again.

Another girl had been put in the room with Sandy and Sarah yesterday. She and Sarah were the same age and they both giggled a lot when Sandy said some things, such as the fact that she was an old woman. They were both good company for Sandy. Carrie was pretty, with beautiful golden hair and hazel eyes. She looked like one of the dolls that Sandy had as a child. She didn't talk much. She was in school with the elders most days and didn't work in the fields or kitchen. She didn't go to classes with Sarah.

Tomorrow was Saturday and there was supposed to be a big feast and meeting because fellow worshipers from the outside were coming in to celebrate that night. Sandy had been assigned to the kitchen to help prepare some of the food and they all had been given new white frocks to wear. She was really excited, as this was the first time since she had been here that she would attend one of these big special events. Everyone said it was beautiful and magical, that you could feel the Divine One's presence, saying that the father spoke directly to him on those nights.

Sandy had heard whispers that there would be a secret ceremony, but only the oldest members would attend that ceremony at the private church in the woods. When she asked, she was told she would find out one day.

Saturday came fast and Sandy was in the kitchen at five in the morning with the others, beginning to cook the food. Sarah came in to help.

"Where's Carrie?" Sandy asked.

"She was chosen for the special ceremony, so she is having prayers with the elder women today," Sarah answered.

Sandy whispered to Sarah, "Do you know what the special ceremony is?"

Sarah shook her head, but she would not look at Sandy.

"Sarah, is something wrong? Tell me."

"Carrie said that once you are chosen, you live somewhere else. I'm going to miss her."

"Well, maybe they just meant somewhere else here in one of the buildings. You'll still see her," Sandy said.

"I know, but she's my best friend and I like her. She makes me really happy."

Sandy hugged Sarah. "I'll be here with you, Sarah, and we'll be sure to visit her. How about that? Does that make you feel better?"

"Okay." Sarah shrugged and then went over to the table where they were shucking corn, offering to help.

"Sandy!" one of the older women called to her. "Go out back and get some more jars of tomatoes for this stew."

"Okay." Sandy headed out to the small cellar in back where they stored more of the vegetables they canned. While in the cellar, she heard voices outside. One of people talking was Mable, one of the elders. She was crying and talking to Sadie, one of the oldest elder women.

"I wish she were a little older. She reminds me so much of my sweet daughter Hattie. Hattie was seventeen when she went to be with the Divine One, but Carrie is only eight. She is so sweet and having her around has been like having my Hattie back."

"I know, Mable, but the father knows who the chosen ones are. He gets his message from the Divine One. So if it's her time, it's her time."

"I know, Sadie. I know."

"Maybe we can ask the father if we can bury her next to Hattie in the chosen garden. My Hattie was special enough to be placed there so she would be with the Divine One in the afterlife." Mable continued to cry.

Sandy sucked in her breath. *Bury*? Carrie was going to die. They were going to kill her.

As her mind started to reel, Sandy thought about what Lydia had said to her one day after she had moved into the main house. She told Sandy she had been chosen but didn't want to go, so she suffered the punishment of the Divine One. That was when she hurt her leg. Sandy wondered to herself. Had they thrown Lydia off a rafter or hurt her long ago for punishment?

Sandy had to do something. She listened and waited until she heard the elder ladies footsteps as they went back inside. Then she waited another five minutes after that before she went in. She wanted to make sure no one had seen her. She went in and put the tomatoes on the table.

When they were told to take a lunch break, she grabbed Sarah and led her outside of the house. "Sarah, I need your help." She told Sarah what she heard and Sarah started to scream. Sandy clamped her hand over Sarah's mouth.

A couple of the elders came toward them, but Sandy said, "We were just playing the sin game." They nodded and walked off.

The sin game was something they did every Sunday. Each person had to name something that would be a sin against the Divine One and then everyone would yell and denounce the sin. Some of them were pretty silly at times, but everyone always chimed in with the yelling. It was sort of cathartic to Sandy and she found that being able to yell like that made her feel better the rest of the day.

This hurting or killing of Carrie was just too much. It was like the last two months had been washed away and reality came flooding back in. She had stifled all her emotions and it was like being slapped in the face. What in the hell was she doing here? How had she been so submissive and brainwashed? These were not good people. They were murderers! She needed to get out of here.

"Sarah, listen to me. We have to get out of her and take Carrie with us."

"You mean leave?" Sarah asked. She was shaking her head no.

"Sarah, didn't you have a family and a place you lived before this? Think, Sarah, think." Sandy was shaking her by the shoulders. Sarah was staring at the ground and starting to cry.

"I had a mommy and daddy and my sister, Rebecca." Sandy could see the realization in her eyes. "I miss them. I want to go home." Sarah continued to cry softly.

Sandy hugged her and pulled her behind one of the sheds. "Good, Sarah, you remember. You cannot say a word to anyone. I have to figure this out before tonight. Will you come with me?" Sandy waited for an answer, as she could see Sarah start to fall apart before her eyes. Crap, what was she doing? Sarah was just a child. What if she told someone?

Sarah looked up at her, her eyes red, but she said in a clear voice, "Yes. I want to go home."

"Good. Let's get something to eat. Then we have to go back in the kitchen and pretend nothing is wrong. After we finish at five o'clock, we have to find Carrie."

When they were back in the kitchen, Sandy tried to not look at Sarah. She was afraid Sarah would cry. Luckily they put Sarah on stew duty and she was cutting up onions and other vegetables, so maybe no one would notice if her eyes kept tearing up.

At exactly five, they were dismissed for personal prayers and to get ready for the service at eight o'clock. Sandy and Sarah ran back to their room, but Carrie wasn't there.

"Let's get dressed and then we'll go look for her," Sandy said.

Sandy knew that even though it was late summer, it would not be dark until later at night. In their white dresses, they would stand out in the dusk and the dark. She looked around and then tore some of the brown drapes off the back window. Sandy got her scissors and cut holes in each one so they were like ponchos they could slip over their heads. She placed then in a sack she could carry.

She and Sarah got dressed and walked out the front door. People were already out in the middle of the compound. People were singing and children playing. It was eerie with everyone in white. The children were spinning around and dancing like flower petals floating on the wind.

Sandy grabbed Sarah's hand and they walked slowly around the compound. They stopped next to each cabin for a minute and listened. Finally, next to Mable's cabin, they heard a laugh. It was Carrie. Sarah looked at Sandy and her grip tightened.

They waited a minute and then darted behind the cabin. One of the windows was slightly open and they could hear talking. It was Mable.

"Carrie, you look beautiful, like a true angel. Now, I want you to sit here and read your good book until I come back for you. Don't talk to anyone."

"Okay, Mother Mable I will," Carrie answered.

They heard the door close and Sandy lifted Sarah up to the window. "Carrie, Carrie," Sarah whispered. "Come over here."

"What are you doing here?" Carrie looked down out of the window at them. "Mother Mable told me not to talk to anyone before the ceremony. She said I should just sit here and read the good book."

"No, Carrie, please, you have to come out here." Sarah had her hand and was pulling.

"No, Sarah. Don't be silly. I'll see you later."

Sarah looked at Sandy and then all of sudden a look came over her. "Carrie, it's about the secret place. I found something. You have to come and see real quickly. It's beautiful. The most beautiful thing I have ever seen!"

"Really, Sarah, what is it?"

"You have to come see it," Sarah said again.

"What about her?" Carrie was looking down at Sandy.

"I didn't tell her. I promise," Sarah said. "I needed Sandy to help me find you. We can go by ourselves and come right back. Sandy will help you back up in the window. No one will ever know you were gone."

Sandy held her breath. She had no idea what Sarah was talking about, so she knew it must be something only Sarah and Carrie shared.

"Okay. I have to be careful of my new dress. Help me down."

Sarah grabbed Carrie's arms and she climbed out and over Sarah and Sandy to get down.

When Sandy saw Carrie's dress, she almost fainted. It was actually a ball gown and it looked store-bought. It was pink satin and she had flowers in her hair. She looked like a little girl going off to a dance.

"Now, Sandy, you cannot follow us. You have to wait right here." Sarah winked at Sandy and then they took off. Sandy could not believe how mature Sarah had become—much different from the frightened little girl she had met on that first day.

Sandy waited a few seconds and then she slowly followed. They were headed over to the east side of the field, where there was a row of fruit trees with green leaves. Sandy had been told those trees provided the best oranges and peaches in the world. She waited behind the last cabin, then took one of the brown drapes out and put it over her head. It was becoming dusk.

The gnats and mosquitos had already started to come out. They were the worst at dusk. In the south, they called some of the gnats "no-see-ums," as they swarmed and repeatedly bit you and you could not see them to swat them. The bites itched right away and for days unless you put something on your skin. The mosquitos actually drew blood when they bit. Sandy had scratched one time until she was covered in welts. They were really biting tonight, but she tried to ignore them and keep focused on following Sarah and Carrie.

As Sandy reached the trees and came out on the other side, she could just barely see Sarah on top of a rock, waving her over that way. Then Sarah jumped down and disappeared.

Sandy got to the rock and went around. She could not see anyone, but then she heard voices. She listened and then realized there was an opening in the rock. It was a cave.

She went in and heard Carrie saying, "I don't see anything new here, Sarah. What are you talking about? Show me now. I have to get back." Then Carrie looked up and saw Sandy.

"You lied to me Sarah." She stomped her foot.

She looked at Sandy and shook her finger. "You're not supposed to be here. This is our secret place."

Sandy looked down and in the faint daylight left, she could see a box. In the box were Barbie dolls, some books, toys, jewelry, colored paper, and other assorted items that she didn't recognize. There were also some candles.

Sarah lit one of the candles. "These are all of the things on the sin list that Mother Mable gave us. She said we are not allowed to have these."

"Where did you get all this stuff?" Sandy asked.

"When new young disciples come to the house, they take all their belongings away to burn," Sarah said. "We knew Mable kept them in a bag until they were burned and we took some of them. We sneak out here and play with them after chores. This is our secret place."

Carrie was turning around to leave. "You tricked me, Sarah. I have to go back. Mother Mable will be mad."

Sarah grabbed her arm. "Carrie, they're going to hurt you."

"No," Carrie said. "I'm going to sleep, and when I wake up, I'll be with the Divine One. Mother Mable told me. It's the greatest honor and gift in the world, and I was specially chosen. You're just jealous." She jerked her arm away from Sarah.

"Carrie, Sandy heard them say it. You'll be dead." Sarah reached out toward her again.

Carrie turned and started to run. Sandy grabbed her and Carrie screamed. "Let me go! Let me go! I'm going back. You're bad. You're both sinners!"

Her screams echoed off the cave walls and Sandy knew she had to do something. Sandy grabbed the sash on Carrie's dress and tore it. Carrie looked at her in disbelief and continued to yell.

"Help me hold her, Sarah. Someone's going to hear." Sarah grabbed Carrie and Sandy gagged her.

"Sarah, we're going to have to tie her up and then go for help. She won't go. She doesn't believe us." Sandy tore more of Carrie's dress and tied her feet and arms. "I'm sorry, Carrie. I know you believe they love you, but I did hear them; you'll be dead after the special ceremony in the woods tonight." Carrie was rolling around and trying to kick.

Sandy gave Sarah a poncho. "We're going to have to run. Maybe they won't find her in here, but I'm sure someone heard her yelling."

They left the cave and could hear voices not too far away. They started to run toward the woods.

"Stay close to that old dirt path over there at the end of the trees. It must go somewhere. Keep running until you find someone. Tell them to call nine-one-one. We need help."

Sarah ran a lot faster than Sandy did and when she turned around to look back, Sandy yelled, "Don't look back. Keep going, no matter what happens!"

The brush was wet from last night's rain and Sandy was starting to get wet. She tripped and fell but got up and ran some more. She could hear voices close behind her and she could see reflections on the trees from flashlights.

She ran and ran and then tripped again. She stood up and felt a hand on her back, then something hit her head; there was a pain in her hip, then nothing.

CHAPTER 26

Detective Carey rubbed his eyes. It had been over two months and there were no new leads on Sandy Milford or the little girls. He was working late again. He had not slept well in weeks.

Sandy's boyfriend, Tom, checked in with him once a week, but he didn't seem as worked up as he had in the beginning. He told Detective Carey he had taken a leave of absence from work and was staying with relatives.

Between his office and the FBI, they had questioned over one hundred people. No leads, no contacts; no one had seen them. The FBI had checked all the fingerprints and evidence from the motel. Everyone had been cleared. Most of the employees had not even had parking tickets.

The only new piece of evidence was when one of the clerks who had quit his job at the motel three months ago had told him the owner had a small dog. So he and the FBI agent had gone back to question her. She said the dog had gotten out and run away. They had been looking everywhere but could not find it. She also told them that a lot of people loved to pet her little dog when they checked in. Her nephew let it stay out in the office and walked it for her. She said it was a brown Chihuahua. They had taken some samples from the owner's apartment, and they matched the hairs found by forensics. That was the only mystery they had solved. At least that explained the brown dog hairs found in Karen's room and on her clothes.

None of the other leads had panned out. The FBI still had the case open and had put an APB out on the woman called "Crazy Betty," but nothing had popped up. They had gotten all kinds of crank callers when they had publicized the pictures of both Betty and the man in black. Some people had called in to say it was Johnny Cash and they had seen him in Nashville or that he was spotted at Comic-con with Vampira, the Queen of Darkness.

It frustrated Sam that people could be so heartless.

Some of the leads seemed plausible, like someone from a 7-Eleven store in a town nearby who said he had seen the man in black. When they went to interview the witness, he could not give a description and the video surveillance system was broken. They drew up a composite based on his description, but it looked more like a ghoul than a real person. The clerk said he had piercing eyes, almost as if he were looking right through him. He still seemed shaken from the encounter with the man in black when they questioned him.

Maybe it really was a man from outer space and they had been taken to another planet. Detective Carey knew people who would probably believe that story. He had met a lot of strange characters in his tenure on the police force, so what some people believed rarely surprised him anymore.

His partner had taken vacation for two weeks to take his children out of town to Florida. He said his girls didn't want to go to the beach here, so Florida seemed like a nice change of pace for them. He had just gotten back today. He had volunteered to stay and work late with Sam.

There had been an increase in the number of complaints from the local citizens about strangers and strange-acting people. All the newspapers had carried the story about Karen and her missing girls. People were scared. He didn't blame them. People should feel safe in their community, but that wasn't the case anymore.

He looked at the pictures on his desk and slammed his hand down. Where the hell were they?

About that time, the desk sergeant stuck his head in the door. "Detective Carey, there's a man on the phone who wants to speak with you. He says it's a matter of life or death."

Sam headed over to his desk and picked up the phone. Chuck saw the look on Sam's face. Sam motioned for Chuck to come over as he continued to talk while writing something down on a pad. "Okay. We're headed that way right now. Can you meet us at the highway intersection?' Sam asked the caller.

"Let's go, Chuck. That was Jake Simmons. He said he knows where the girls are and that we need to go now." Detective Carey stood up and checked his gun. "I'll grab some of the other officers on the way out."

"I can't let you do that, Sam," Chuck said.

"What the hell are you talking about, Chuck? Didn't you hear what I said?"

Sam turned around toward Chuck and was stunned to see that Chuck had his gun drawn.

"I can't let you go, Sam. You'll destroy my family and ruin my little girls' lives. The father has been good to us. He promised my wife and me we could keep our little girls at home and he and his disciples would pay for them to go to college. He said one of my girls needed to be a lawyer and the other one a doctor to help serve the Divine One. You'll ruin it all. I can't let that happen. My family is all I have. I would give my life for them. You have to understand. The only way is the way of the Divine One. I have kept my promise to the father and kept all of his followers safe. Those missing girls are better off with him. Their mother was a sinner. She paraded them around like whores in those costumes. She deserved to be punished." Chuck took aim at Sam's head.

Just then the desk sergeant opened the door and Chuck turned his head slightly. Sam rushed him and Chuck's gun went off. Sam and Chuck struggled and they both fell to the floor and continued to wrestle for control of the weapon. The gun fired again. Sam fell back and Chuck went limp.

"What the hell?" The desk sergeant rushed in and grabbed Sam.

"No time to explain," Sam said. "Chuck was in on it all. He helped cover up the kidnappings and the missing girls. He knew all about it. We have to go now. I know where the missing girls are."

Jan Sylve

"We have to call someone. You can't leave," The desk sergeant said. "You know the rules, Sam. There needs to be an investigation about what happened here. I can't just take your word for it. For God's sake, Chuck was your partner." He started toward Sam.

"Then you'll have to shoot me; I'm going," Sam said. He slugged the desk sergeant and ran out the door as he fell to the floor.

Other officers were running toward the room as Sam ran down the hall and made it out the front door. He reached his car, started it and squealed tires as he drove off. Multiple officers were running out of the building and Sam knew they would follow. He just had to outrun them and get there before they could stop him.

CHAPTER 27

Sandy slowly opened her eyes. She couldn't remember a time when she had felt so weak and exhausted. She tried to recall what had happened. Vaguely, she remembered running in wet clothes through the woods, falling many times, getting back up and running some more. Her hip was painful and beginning to throb like a toothache. Her head hurt. Suddenly, she realized she was up high in the air and something was around her neck. Her feet felt cold as if she was standing on some type of metal. Her hands were tied against her sides, but she could reach her hip with her fingers.

As she rubbed her hip, a muffled voice said, "Those tranquilizer darts hurt a bit, don't they? We use them on the deer."

Sandy looked up and could see all the hooded figures in the faint light coming through the cracks in the shed's wooden slats. They were all swaying in unison and humming or maybe that was just the buzzing in her head. She saw a single figure walk toward the shed door with a gold book held high in their hand. When she heard the voice, she knew it was him.

The Father began to read louder and louder as he reached the shed and kicked the door open. He didn't even pause and with one swift kick the ladder beneath her was gone.

Sandy's last thoughts were of Sarah and Carrie and then she saw her Mom's figure in a flash of light as she felt the noose tighten around her neck.

CHAPTER 28

Sandy thought she was dreaming. She heard voices and could feel someone holding her. She opened her eyes to find that an elderly man with gray hair and overalls had her in his arms.

"You're going to be okay, honey. I've got you," The man was crying as he spoke.

Sandy looked up and shook her head back and forth to indicate no to him. She tried to speak, but her throat was so sore. She reached up to touch her throat but her arm fell back down. She was so very weak.

"Just wait, honey," the man said to her. "An ambulance is coming for you."

She was on the ground and as she looked past him, she saw blue lights and cars with uniformed men. Police! Behind one of the cars Sandy could see that the main house was on fire, people were screaming, and then she heard gunshots off in the distance. She saw some of the women running and others falling down on the ground wailing.

Then she heard a ruckus off to the left and a man yelling, "Let me see her! Let me see her!" *Tom.* That was Tom's voice. She tried to turn her head and in the light, she could see him. She tried to mouth his name. A police officer was pulling him back. What was wrong?

"You whore of Babylon! You ruined it all. They're taking the father and my whole family to jail. You've destroyed everything, you sinner! You will burn in hell!" That was Tom's voice.

Tears started running down her face. That couldn't be Tom. What was wrong with him?

The man holding her spoke. "He came here looking for you. He loved you. I tried to help him, but once his family knew he was here, they got to him. All of these people are part of his mother's family. I'm his Uncle Jake. I rescued his mother from this life years ago and never told a soul where she was for years. I smuggled her out to meet the man she loved and he took her away from all of this. She never really belonged here. She was much too innocent and sweet. She was a beautiful soul and my baby sister. I just couldn't let this happen to her. She found the strength to come back and face them once. That is when they truly knew then she was lost to them forever. I believe if she had known what this new preacher, the Father, was up to then she would have told the police. Her family did not want to risk her finding out, so they let her go and considered her lost to them. What is really strange is that strength his Mom had come from her belief in God. So many of my kin strayed from the righteous path and became the crazy zealots that live here now. Deep down, I knew, but I just couldn't face what they had become. I am really, really sorry Sandy," his voice shook now and he sobbed as he held her.

"This has been my family's life for a hundred years. There has always been a 'father' here. I grew up with it. My dad was a minister, but he wasn't like this man. He was strict, but also kind and loving. He said that family must always stick together. We only have each other against the rest of the world. There's so much evil and sin out there. Things were good back then and only those who wanted to join our way voluntarily became followers.

When Ezra, the man you call the father, came he ingratiated himself into the family and my dad accepted him as a true believer. When my dad died, he took over. He convinced my family that he was truly long lost kin. The woman he came with, Betty, really was a distant cousin of ours.

When Tom showed up down here, that is when I knew they had taken you. I thought I could find a way to help get you out of here. I was trying to buy some time and keep him safe. The father got to him and slowly brainwashed him, just like he did to most of my family. I used to be an elder with the church, but when the father took over our group, I quit. It all just went wrong from there on out. I stayed because of my wife. She loved the father. After she died, I just kept to myself.

Believe me I never knew they were taking girls and women until just recently. I never came out here. I kept to myself, but my sin is that I kept my mouth shut. When Tom came looking for you and I heard what happened at the motel, I realized the whole truth. I'll have to answer to God and the authorities for keeping this evil secret."

"How did you find me?" Sandy asked. Her throat hurt and her voice was barely above a whisper.

"I heard about the big ceremony tonight from the boys talking at Sadie's house. I was afraid you were the innocent lamb to be sacrificed they were talking about. I will never understand how this lunatic, "the Father," convinced my family that any human must be offered to the Divine One for his followers to be blessed. I started thinking about Tom's Mom and how I rescued her from this life all those years ago. Something just came over me. I headed this way not knowing for sure what I would do. When I was driving down the road, Sarah came running out of the woods screaming. She told me what was going on and I called Detective Carey on my cell phone. I gave him directions and met him out at the main turn off to the road. We drove up just as everyone was converging on this shed. Detective Carey shot the rope just after you fell from the ladder. All hell broke loose then with lights and sirens as all the other policemen got here. There was a lot of shooting and the father is dead." Jake hung his head. "Some of the elders set the house on fire and barricaded themselves inside. You were passed out for several minutes. I was starting to worry if you would make it, but you were breathing. I prayed for you."

Behind him, she saw ambulance lights and fire trucks beginning to surround the main house. The police officers were pointing and yelling as they grabbed some of the hooded figures.

"Forgive me," Jake said. That was the last thing Sandy heard him say as the police came forward and pulled him up. "We have a lot of questions for you mister." They dragged him away.

Ambulance attendants were running toward her and one now kneeled down beside her and placed an oxygen mask on her face.

CHAPTER 29

Two weeks later, Sandy was sitting on a plane. She had called her boss at the bank. They had read the newspaper reports and seen the coverage on national TV. The bank gave her back a job along with a bonus. She had asked the bank manager if she could be transferred out to California. She just could not face going back to Denver. He said he understood and he would help in any way she needed. All of her fellow employees at the bank had either called, sent cards or flowers. The two girls she was good friends with at the bank had called and talked to her several times. They both promised they would come and visit in California. None of them could believe what had happened or that Tom had turned against her.

The bank arranged to have all her belongings shipped to San Francisco from storage. Since Sandy had been paid up on rent for a year, her landlord who was a nice elderly man had put then in storage when she didn't return. He had even reported her missing. Sandy had called him and written him a nice letter. It made her feel really good there were kind people like that still in the world.

Sandy had not read the papers or watched the news on TV for the last two days. She declined all interviews in the hospital. The police had placed a guard at her door while she was in the hospital recovering from the bruising and swelling to her throat.

She had gotten a letter from Uncle Jake. It was delivered by a police officer. Jake wished her God speed and blessings in a new life. He wrote in the letter that the day he rescued her was the day he was truly saved. He went on to say again how sorry he was about Tom. He emphasized in the letter that his family had spent so much time convincing Tom while he was staying with them that she was really a bad person. Jake wrote that the family told Tom that only a jezebel would run away and leave a man she truly loved. They brainwashed him to believe they, his family, were all about love, honesty and truth. Jake added that the Father had a way of getting through to even the most educated, rational people. Jake had witnessed that more than once over the years. He wrote that Tom, being an only child, fell in quickly with his new found family. He ended the letter by writing that Tom was lost to both of them now. Sandy cried for an hour when she finished reading the letter.

She still could completely wrap her head around the fact that Tom had turned against her. She went over and over it in her mind. Was there something about him as a person that she had missed? How could she have loved a man who could be brainwashed so easily? She had loved him for his kindness and strength. Also, when he spoke about his parents, she could tell the deep love and respect he had for them. How on earth could a man like that turn on someone he professed to love?

She accepted that she had to find a way to let go of those thoughts and move on with her life. Maybe there was something in his psyche that wasn't apparent on the surface. She thought about what she had often heard; you never truly know someone one hundred percent. There are always some character flaws that remain hidden and come out in the worst of times. Well, this had absolutely been the worst of times. After this experience, Sandy knew that she would always be a little more suspicious and cautious of any man in the future. Actually, she would be wary of any person for that matter, man or woman.

Tom was in jail now with all the elders, including his aunts and uncles. The whole family would be going to trial. Sandy was told by the police that she might have to come back for the trial, but the prosecuting attorney had already petitioned for a change of venue; since there were so many relatives in this county, he didn't see how they could pick a non-biased jury. The attorney told her she would have plenty of notice if and when she was needed. It could take months just to gets the case on a docket since there was so much publicity surrounding the events that took place.

Sandy had videotaped all of her testimony and also signed the transcribed copies before she got on the plane to leave South Carolina.

Rebecca, Sarah, and Carrie had been picked up by their families and Sandy was told by the police that they had arranged for all of them to be placed in psychiatric counseling at the cost of the state. They had offered that for all the victims and families, including her.

Sarah's grandmother had come by to see Sandy once before the family left town. She said Rebecca still blamed them for taking her away from the father. She told Sandy all of the family knew it would take a long time for them to see any semblance of the little girls they had all known before this happened. She hugged Sandy and thanked her for being there for her daughter's children. Sarah had told all of them how much Sandy had helped take care of them. Sarah was doing better than Rebecca, but she still was having nightmares and crying a lot.

Sarah's grandmother also told Sandy she had met the parents of both Lila and Mary. They had told her the girls were still speaking very little to anyone. The parents had promised to keep in touch with her and let her know how they were doing. She said they had all bonded together during the sessions with the police family counselors. She exchanged phone numbers with Sandy. Sandy would call sometime and see how the girls were doing.

Detective Carey visited Sandy a couple of times after she got out of the hospital and stayed around to give the video testimony. He had arranged a safe house for her to stay in, so she felt protected and comfortable. He repeatedly said to her that he was so sorry this had happened to her. He told her about the makeshift jail in the back of the owner's apartment at the motel. That fact had ended up making it in all the papers, but not all the details were released. He told her in confidence, as he felt like she should know that the little girls had been right when they said they were in a jail. He told Sandy there had been a secret door behind the bookshelf. Some of the missing persons from years past turned out to be part of the followers they arrested and now considered themselves to be true believers. Most had been children or young woman when they had been taken who were adults now and considered accomplices to the father. They had been victims at one time, so the FBI was still trying to decide what should be done with them. They were also being given counseling and their families had been contacted.

Sam told Sandy it had really shaken his faith in people to know there were generations of a whole family here in his town capable of doing such things.

He told her ten of the adults and some children had died in the house fire. They were still trying to identify all of them. Mable and Sadie Simmons had been among them. Most had died from smoke inhalation in their rooms. Jake had identified the two women's bodies.

Sandy felt sorry for most of the disciples. She surprised even herself that she could feel any compassion toward any of them considering how they had helped the father continue to kidnap women and girls over the years. The majority of the older girls had been sweet to her and all the children. Hearing from Sam about the loss of a few of the children in the fire really did break her heart. She knew there were many families out there hoping for news about their children, only to find out they were lost to them in the end because of the madness of a whole group of people and one truly insane man.

Jan Sylve

Sandy had hugged Detective Carey when he left. She told him there were no words to describe how she felt. She told him she knew it was his job, but the fact he never gave up and risked his life was more than any other person she knew on earth would have done for a stranger. She had overheard one of the policemen at the safe house say, "Detective Carey sure put his life and career on the line for this one." When Sandy asked the policeman directly what he meant, he told her he could not discuss it.

CHAPTER 30

Internal Affairs cleared Sam of any wrongdoing in the death of his partner.

Sam was still grieving and angry at the same time about it all. It was hard for him to accept that he had worked side by side with Chuck for years and the whole time he was protecting those lunatics out there at that farm. Maybe it was the difference in the way he was raised and had grown up. Sam's family was close and maybe he might take a bullet for one of them, but never commit a crime or protect them if they broke the law. Right was right and wrong was wrong.

No matter how strong family bonds were, it never justified destroying other peoples' lives. He loved his family, but he would not and could not accept that he would protect them if they were criminals or murderers.

Chuck had died from his wounds and also had been stripped of his police honors. His wife was in jail with the other family members. Chuck's daughters had been sent to live with his parents. The FBI determined that his daughters and the paternal grandparents had no knowledge of what Chuck's wife's cousins were doing.

The manager from the motel had cracked under interrogation. Once he had been arrested and realized he was facing jail time, he started to confess about the events surrounding Karen's death. He said he had spiked Karen's tea at dinner on the night Sandy had seen her at the bar. She had left the two girls in the room watching TV, so he had decided that was the best time to kidnap them. The father had picked Karen's little girls out of a whole group in Charleston and told his followers that he knew which girls were special and chosen ones. He told his flock that the Divine One led him to these special two little girls. Over the years the father had singled out certain women and girls in his travels. He said he knew they were chosen to do God's bidding. He just had to bring them into the fold and show them the way.

The motel manager said they had taken Karen and the girls out of their room later that night. There was a false wall from the storage room into the back of the closet in the motel room where they were staying. Karen woke up sooner than they expected and started yelling and banging on the walls in the makeshift jail. His other cousin, Joe, had put a sheet around her neck to scare her and lead her to another room to make her be quiet. Joe accidentally choked her to death. The motel manager said his cousin had panicked, so they took her back to her room and hung her from the door to make it look like a suicide.

The father was mad at them and told them they should be punished for bringing attention to the motel and getting the police involved. The father also told them that Karen needed to be replaced, so that is when they drugged Sandy and took her. They thought she was just another tourist in town by herself, someone no one would miss right away. The manager had noted when she checked in that she was from Colorado. Somewhere that was really far off.

While listening to the motel manager's confession, Detective Carey thought to himself that this guy wasn't the brightest in the world. Sam was really surprised that this guy had been able to pull this off in the past with other women who had gone missing. The manager was only thirty-five years old and Sam knew he would be in jail for the rest of his life. At least he hoped that was the case.

Sam considered them all sick individuals who had been led by an insane man, the so-called father, who convinced them it was all in the name of some Divine being guiding him directly. Detective Carey had told her the whole story when he visited her for the last time at the safe house. He had shaken her hand when he left and said, "I'm glad you made it. You're really remarkable and one of the bravest women I have ever met. You're one of the lucky ones."

Sandy looked out the plane window and saw that the sun was coming up. It was the beginning of a new day for her and it truly was the most beautiful sunrise she had ever seen. She was going to make the most of her new life.

ABOUT THE AUTHOR

Ms. Sylve spent her childhood growing up in the South. She traveled every summer with her family to different states across the country, but her heart belonged to the simple small town life and the history that was handed down from families for generations. She was taught to respect her elders and their Southern traditions. Family was the most important thing above all else.

The roots of her origin stuck with her throughout her life and her travels around the world. She was fascinated with the mysteries that accompanied each culture she experienced and the determination of the people to preserve past practices, no matter how archaic they might seem to outsiders.

Each foreign country demonstrated a dedication to preserve their past and a special reverence for their elders. One country's tradition might include black magic while another culture demonstrated a staunch dedication to centuries old religious practices. In many lands there existed a blind dedication to a certain belief or faith and there was no acceptance of anything outside of that realm. Those beliefs held a certain fascination for her.

Ms. Sylve worked as a professional before retiring from the federal government. Often a mystery presented itself in ordinary day-to-day life. She often marveled at what could be gleaned from a casual conversation or a passing comment from a stranger. All people need a touch of mystery in their lives, but many people fear what they cannot understand or grasp.

Printed in the United States
By Bookmasters